THE SCAR BOYS

THE SCAR BOYS

A NOVEL

LEN VLAHOS

USA

NEW YORK

EGMONT

We bring stories to life

First published by Egmont USA, 2014
443 Park Avenue South, Suite 806
New York, NY 10016

1 3 5 7 9 8 6 4 2

www.egmontusa.com
www.lenvlahos.com

Library of Congress Cataloging-in-Publication Data

Vlahos, Len.
The Scar Boys : a novel / Len Vlahos.
pages cm
Summary: Written as a college admission essay, eighteen-year-old Harry Jones
recounts a childhood defined by the hideous scars he hid behind, and how form-
ing a band brought self-confidence, friendship, and his first kiss.
ISBN 978-1-60684-439-7 (hardcover) [1. Disfigured persons—Fiction.
2. Friendship—Fiction. 3. Bands (Music)—Fiction. 4. Near-death experiences—
Fiction. 5. Family life—Fiction. 6. New York (State)—Fiction.] I. Title.
PZ7.V854Sc 2014
[Fic]—dc23
2013018265

Printed in the United States of America

For Kristen, Charlie, and Luke—you are my music.

Please write an essay of 250 words on a topic of your choice. Your personal essay will help us become acquainted with you beyond your courses, grades, and test scores. It will also demonstrate your ability to organize your thoughts and express yourself in writing. You may choose to write about your interest in attending our university, your goals or career plans, a significant community service experience, a person who has influenced your life, a challenge you have had to overcome, or any other special information or circumstances that may assist us in the admissions process. We look forward to getting to know you better.

_____

_____

_____

_____

_____

_____

_____

_____

_____

_____

_____

January 21, 1987

The University of Scranton
Office of Undergraduate Admissions
Scranton, PA 18510-4699

Dear Admissions Professional,

Thank you for giving me the opportunity to become
a matriculating student at the University of Scranton. I have had many interesting experiences in
my life. I will represent the school well. I work
hard and am a quick study. I have a wide variety
of interests and I am dedicated to--Wait.

Wait, wait, wait.

250 words? Are you kidding? It can't be done.
Whoops, just wasted four words, five if you count
the contraction, telling you "it can't be done."
Another 17 words talking about telling you that
"it can't be done." Another 12 . . . never mind. This
could go on forever.

Here's the short version of what you need to know:

I'm ugly and shy and my face, head, and neck
are covered with hideous scars. (15 words)

Here's the slightly longer version:

I'm ugly and shy and my face, head, and neck are covered with hideous scars.

I was almost struck by lightning.

I wish I had been struck by lightning.

I was a methadone addict before the age of 10.

It's my fault that my best friend almost got killed.

I played guitar in the greatest punk rock band you've never heard of.

And that was all before my 19th birthday, which isn't for another five months. (76 words)

But the most important thing to know about me, what you really need to grok in order to understand what kind of student you'll be getting, is that I, Harbinger Robert Francis Jones, am a coward.

I just counted and "coward" was word number 248, and that doesn't even include the date or your address, so I should stop. But I can't believe you know me any better yet, and that was your goal, right? So with your permission--strike that, with or without your permission--I'm going to exceed that word count, just a little.

Okay, maybe a lot.

I suppose I should start at the beginning, and it begins with a question . . .

THUNDER ROAD

(written by Bruce Springsteen, and performed by Bruce Springsteen and the E Street Band)

"Who the fuck are you?"

An older and much larger boy stood over me, blotting out the sun. "You weren't god damn here when we chose up the god damn sides." He was trying on curse words the way a little girl tries on her mother's shoes.

The boy wasn't just big, he was cartoon big. He also wasn't alone. He was one of seven snot-nosed tweens surrounding me like I was in the middle of a football huddle. They had decided to make me a central character in their game of Ringolevio. I had no idea what that word meant, and didn't have a clue about the rules of the game, but near as I could tell, it was something between hide-and-seek and all-out neighborhood war.

I don't remember what I was doing just before the "Who the fuck are you?" It's as if the entire universe came into being all at once in that exact moment. Earlier memories just don't exist for me. Strike that. They exist, but they're buried in a place where I can't find them. They can only be reconstructed from the outside. (If you're wondering how this can be, give yourself a pat on the back, because you're asking a really good question. Read on.)

"Who the fuck are you?" the boy demanded a second time.

A thick haze hung between the sun and Earth like gauze, trying to choke the life out of everything—even the flies and mosquitoes didn't have any energy. It was the kind of summer afternoon that bred impatience.

"I don't know," I muttered back. With no brothers or sisters to properly weave me to the fabric of kid society, I was, at eight years old, mostly overlooked, and only occasionally tolerated by the other children in our neighborhood. I was so lost in the excitement of an older boy actually talking to me, that it took me a minute to realize it wasn't going so well.

"You don't know who you are? Are you fucking retarded, shit-for-brains?" The other boys laughed.

"I'm Harry Jones," I mumbled at my shoes.

"Well then," the older boy said and puffed out his chest like Patton, "you, Harry Shit Jones, have been caught by the Sharks—that's our team—and you're our prisoner." The other boys stomped their feet in approval. I'd wandered into the final act of *Lord of the Flies* but was too young to know it. "And what's worse, you little ass head," he leaned in close, "you've been caught cheating."

"I wasn't chea—"

"Shut up."

"Honest, I wasn't—"

He punched me, hard, in the shoulder. I was already too scared to cry, and somehow I knew crying would only make it worse. *Maybe if I take my lumps,* I thought, *it'll all turn out okay.*

"Whaddya think we should do with him?" someone asked.

One of the other kids, a freckled little creep named Timmy, who called me "Shrimp Toast" every time he saw me playing in front of my house, was holding a length of rope, maybe a clothesline, maybe something else. "I think we should put him in *jail*," he said. This was met with laughs and hoots all around.

The jail was a small but sturdy dogwood tree, its thick green leaves providing shade, but no protection from the heat. According to the rules, I was supposed to keep one hand on the tree at all times until a teammate tagged me free. But I didn't know the rules, didn't know rope wasn't supposed to be part of the game.

I let them tie me to the tree without a struggle, never complaining as they pulled the nylon cord too tight, wrapping it several times around the trunk, binding me from my shoulders to my knees.

Thick gray clouds soon replaced the summer haze, and the painfully still air started to move. The first drops of rain prompted one mother after another to open her ranch house window and bellow for little Jimmy or Johnny or Danny to get inside. The game started to break as the kids sprinted for home. No one seemed to remember I was there, bound to that tree.

"Guys!" I screamed. "GUYS!"

Childhood, for all its good press, is a time when the human animal explores the dark side of the Force, pushing the limit of the pain it's willing to inflict on bugs, squirrels, and little neighborhood boys. Most kids outgrow the darker impulses by high school. The ones that don't spend their teenage years playing football, lacrosse, and, dating the prom queen. (It doesn't seem fair to me, either, but hey, I don't make the rules.)

Only one boy, Timmy with the freckles and the rope, heard me. He turned around and we locked eyes. I believed, if only for an instant, that I was saved. By the time I understood why his face was twisting itself into something between a smile and sneer, he was already in a dead run, headed for his own house, probably planning to torture his hamster or sister or something. I heard his door slam shut.

The first bolt of lightning wasn't a bolt at all. It was

a flash, like a camera's flash, bringing every atom of the world into stark relief for a nanosecond. My mother taught me to count "Mississippis" when I saw lightning, so I did. There were nine before I heard the first rumble of thunder. I forgot what that meant, but I knew the heart of the storm was still far away, and as long as there were at least nine in the next group of Mississippis, I'd be safe.

The rain started falling harder, the noise surrounding me like freeway traffic. There was another flash and I started to count again.

One Mississippi. The wind was blowing little pieces of our neighborhood across the lawn: an unsecured lid from a plastic garbage can, a red kickball, a white dress shirt liberated from someone's untended clothesline.

Two Mississippi. A latticework fence supporting tomato plants was bending sideways as the rain, now waving in translucent sheets like see-through shower curtains, pooled into muddy lakes around the yard. My brain turned to jelly and my bladder let loose.

Three Mississi—a sonic BOOM slammed my head against the tree. My skin and clothes were drenched in a cocktail of rainwater, sweat, and urine. The heart of the storm—now a living, breathing thing—had moved closer.

Another flash and I started my count again, this time out loud.

"One Mississippi!" My voice, choked by its own sobs, only carried a few feet forward where it was swallowed by the torrent of water and wind. I began writhing like a fish on a hook, trying to loosen the nylon cord and slip free.

"Two Mississippi!" I noticed a cat, its tortoiseshell hair matted flat by the deluge, hiding beneath a stack of lawn chairs that was pushed up against the house in front of me. Its legs were pulled tight under its waterlogged body, and its eyes were open wide, darting back and forth and looking for some escape. It spotted me, held my gaze, and wailed like a banshee, loud enough for me to hear through the rain.

"Three Mississippi!" Seeing the cat calmed me down. I wasn't alone. As long as we were together, me and this cat, we were going to be okay. I regained control of my voice. The wind died down just a little. Even the fence with the tomato plants wasn't bending so far forward.

"Four Mississippi!" No lightning. No thunder. The storm was moving away.

"Five Mississippi!" I thought I could hear my mom's voice calling me. She sounded far away and she sounded scared. I tried to call back, but my voice still wasn't carrying. I shouted again, as loud as I could: "MOM!"

"Six Missi—" Before I could say "ssippi," before any thunder from that flash reached my ears, and before I had any idea if my mother heard me calling out to her, a new spear of lightning found me. It struck the tree just above my head.

In the instant before everything went black, just before I was sure I'd died, I looked up and saw that the cat was gone.

SOMEBODY GET ME A DOCTOR

(written by Eddie Van Halen, Alex Van Halen, Michael Anthony, and David Lee Roth, and performed by Van Halen)

The lightning bolt sawed the top of the tree cleanly off. A large shaft of the trunk, a piece like a battering ram, landed on my head. It fractured my skull, dislocated my shoulder, and knocked me unconscious. What was left of the tree—enough that I was still loosely bound to it— caught fire, leaving third-degree burns on my shoulders, neck, face, and scalp. My mother found me dangling there in just enough time to pull me free, call an ambulance, and save my life.

I didn't remember any of it.

I woke up four days later in a dimly lit hospital room that smelled like Bactine. Whirring machines and blinking lights formed an eerie halo around my body, pieces of which, including my face, were wrapped in gauze. My view of the world was restricted to a small, cotton-framed slit.

At first I was disoriented. I wondered if I was on a submarine or a spaceship. But as soon as I tried to move, the pain went coursing through the millions of exposed nerve endings, and I passed out. I regained and lost consciousness like that often the first couple of weeks.

The treatments during my "recovery" were the kind of nightmare from which you just can't wake up. The worst of it was the changing of the bandages. The nurses tried to make it a game by calling it the Changing of the Guard. "You know Harry, like at Buckingham Palace." Only I didn't know what Buckingham Palace was, and even if I had known, it wouldn't have helped. The balm slathered on my wounds acted like glue, fusing the sterilized cotton pads to the fleshy meat of my neck and head, leaving the nurses with no choice but to rip the bandages off. And when I say "rip," I mean they would grab an end of the gauze and pull it like they were trying to start a gas-powered lawn mower. I would put up such a fight that they had to strap me down. They had me on a morphine drip for most of my hospital stay, and I took an oral version of methadone hydrochloride for many months after. It was supposed to help manage the pain in a less addictive way. It didn't entirely work.

My memory of the doctors and nurses is colored by images of generals and admirals—a group of authoritative yahoos trying to inspire me back to full health, telling me to "buck up," to "be brave," to "never give up hope." I lost count of how many times they told me it was a miracle I wasn't killed and that I should be grateful to have spent only forty-five days in the hospital. They had no answer for the burns, which, while they did heal, left me badly and irrevocably scarred, or for my memory loss, which left gaping holes in my personal history that had to be rebuilt by others.

By the time I got home, I was inconsolable. People talk about the resiliency of children, but those same people have never tied those same children to a tree during a thunderstorm to test the theory. I refused to eat, refused to speak, even refused to watch television. My parents tried all manner of carrots and sticks to coax me out of my funk, but nothing worked.

Nothing until I met Lucky Strike the Lightning Man.

Years earlier, Lucky had been working as a groundskeeper on an estate north of where we lived when a wayward thread of lightning struck him on the top of the head.

It was something between a miracle and a fluke that Lucky's injuries were as minor as they were. He spent eighteen hours unconscious, and woke up with a mild headache and strange gaps in his memory. For example, he couldn't remember the name of his cat, so he eventually renamed it "Bolt." The cat, Lucky would tell me, never answered to the new name. It seemed instead to be waiting for someone, anyone, to call it by its proper name. No one ever did.

Lucky found himself spending every free minute reading about lightning, researching storm systems, and attending meteorology classes at the local community college. He needed to understand how and why he'd been singled out. Lightning became his great white whale.

Through this obsession, Lucky met and was embraced by an underground network of natural disaster fanatics—tornado chasers, earthquake junkies, hurricane watchers, even one lonely devotee of tsunamis. When they founded the Society for the Study of Natural Phenomena, it was no surprise that Lucky—the only one of the group to have experienced his natural disaster firsthand—was asked to serve as the group's president.

The first official function of Nat-Phen, as they called themselves, was a presentation at a local library on the dangers of weather. Using blowups of photographs and acetate slides shone on a mammoth screen, the session—titled *Hurricanes, Tornadoes, and Lightning: What You Don't Know Just Might Kill You*—was a smashing success. The *Putnam County Weekly* called it "an eye-opening, hair-raising ride," and singled out "Lucky Strike the Lightning Man" as a "fellow who knows his stuff." Other libraries caught wind of the group, and Nat-Phen was invited to give a series of presentations all around southern New York State.

My mother read about one of Lucky's presentations, and that was how he and I met.

Lucky was tall and lean and had a thick mane of blond hair with one shock of gray arching up from his forehead. His eyes bulged out of their sockets, and he had a slight quiver to his thin lower lip. The rosy hue of his cheeks stood out against the ghostly pallor of his skin. I thought maybe he was a teacher or a professor because his tweed blazer had patches sewn on the sleeves.

I wondered if Lucky was disappointed that I wasn't actually struck by lightning, that I was hit by a falling, burning tree struck by lightning. In a lot of ways my life would've been easier if I'd received a direct hit. To be the boy *almost* struck by lightning was like finishing second in the big race. You ran, but no one cared. But if Lucky was disappointed, he didn't let it show.

"Had the lightning hit you directly," he told me, "your burns probably would have been much less severe." He had a very civilized way of speaking, like a career diplomat, like Winchester from *M*A*S*H*. "That's not to say you would have come through unscathed. Electricity flows through a human body, which, unlike a tree, is quite a good conductor of current. It is like being inside a microwave oven, for just an instant." Microwaves weren't all that common in 1976, but I knew what they were and I formed a mental image of bubbling soup.

"The concentrated surge of energy," he continued, "eviscerates the nervous and autonomic systems." I didn't know what *eviscerate* meant or what *autonomic systems* were, but he had my attention. "Our brethren, those souls fortunate enough to survive a lightning strike, often suffer terrible maladies."

"Maladies?" I asked, sounding out the word

"Illnesses," he answered.

"Like what?"

"Oh, from simple things like headaches, dizziness, and vomiting, to more serious ailments like amnesia, depression, and suicide. In very brutal strikes," he said, "the heart can stop, depriving the brain of blood and oxygen. When it restarts, the victim is something of a vegetable. No, wait," he smiled, "not a vegetable, a piece of toast."

My mother, who'd been sitting quietly in a corner of the room, got quickly to her feet. I guess talking about depression and suicide to an already distraught eight-year-old wasn't what she had in mind when she invited Lucky to our house. But then Mom looked at me and saw something in my eyes—a spark of life, a flicker of hope, or maybe just plain old interest—that she hadn't seen since before the storm.

The truth is my mom's a saint. She sacrificed everything for me after the storm. She used to play tennis, she used to be in bowling leagues, hell, my mom used to write. All of that went up in smoke with me and that dogwood tree.

It took me a couple of years to figure out how much the lightning strike had been affecting the people around me, and when I did I felt awful. Mom saw me moping more than usual one day and asked what was wrong.

"Nothing," I said.

"No, really honey, what is it?"

"I'm just sorry is all."

"Sorry for what?"

"For ruining your life." I have a flair for the dramatic when I want to, but I meant what I said. I really did.

Mom looked at me and burst into tears. "Don't ever, ever, ever apologize again," she said to me. "Never." She hugged me and held on to me for as long as I would let her, which that day was a long time.

So when my mom saw me connecting with Lucky, or rather, saw Lucky connecting with me, she knew enough to let it play out. She sat back down.

"A piece of toast?" I asked Lucky. He nodded, and then shifted gears.

"Do you know, young man," he asked, "what can happen when one little butterfly flaps its wings in China, all the way on the other side of the world?"

I didn't, so I shook my head.

"When those little wings flap," and here he extended

his gangly arms and made slow, graceful flapping motions, "they move little molecules in the air. Do you know what molecules are?"

I was pretty sure I did, so I nodded.

"Good, good. Now picture those molecules moving and bumping into other molecules, which bump into other molecules, which bump into other molecules. All these molecules affecting the course of those that surround them, changing them, moving them in different directions, just because a butterfly flapped its wings." He could see I was confused. "So a butterfly flapping its wings in China in April can cause a thunderstorm in New York in July," he finished.

I thought about this. Was Lucky trying to tell me that my thunderstorm was caused by a butterfly in China? Or was he telling me that things like thunderstorms are so random that there's no point trying to make sense of them?

"You see, Harry, even the tiniest little event, something that can happen so quickly that you would miss it were you to blink your eyes, can have long-lasting, far-reaching consequences. One little thing can cause so many other things to happen. And here is the secret." He leaned in so close I could smell the aftershave on his neck and the peppermint chewing gum on his breath. "All these things that happen, if you don't control them, they will control you. It is up to you, Harry." He held my gaze for a moment, waiting to see if I understood. I wasn't sure I did, though I knew what he was telling me was important.

Lucky took my hand in his and told me to keep my chin up. I took him literally, and despite the pain of healing burns and structural damage to my neck, I managed to sit up a little straighter. With that he got up to go.

He left me a card with his phone number and told me I could call him at any time for any reason. "We are brothers," he said, "brothers of the storm."

I never saw Lucky again, and I never called the number, but I've carried that card with me my entire life. It's like a Valium prescription, always at the ready, just in case.

BAD BRAIN

(written by Dee Dee Ramone, Joey Ramone, Johnny Ramone,
and Marky Ramone, and performed by the Ramones)

Life after the lightning strike was a blur of car rides and waiting rooms. I was shuttled from neurologists, to infectious disease specialists, to plastic surgeons. Teams of doctors floated over me and tried to fix my broken body. They stuck me with hypos and IVs to fight the bacteria nesting in my wounds, they used low-level electric stimulation to repair my damaged nerves, and they performed countless surgeries in a vain attempt to make me look like someone's idea of "normal." I was Steve Austin, the Six Million Dollar Man. Only I wasn't, because the whole thing turned out to be a big fat waste of time.

Well, mostly.

Dr. Kenneth Hirschorn, or Dr. Kenny as I came to know him, was young and edgy; he had longish hair, wore his shirt untucked, and had Sharpie drawings of rock stars ringing the walls of his office. He was a pediatric psychiatrist and his assignment was to wean me off the pain meds to which I'd become addicted. He would talk to me about Lou Reed, Janis Joplin, Syd Barrett, and any other rock star he could think of who had abused drugs.

"By getting off the junk now, Harry," and yes, Dr. Kenny taught me to call it *junk*, "you're already way cooler than they ever were." I was probably the only kid my age to know all the words to the Velvet Underground's "I'm Waiting for the Man." He guided me through the misery of controlled withdrawal like a shaman initiating a warrior in the ways of battle.

It was dumb luck, Faceless Admissions Professional, that Dr. Kenny and I found each other. ("Faceless Admissions Professional" is a heck of a mouthful. Okay if I just call you FAP for short? Good, thanks.) If I'd been sent to any other psychiatrist, I would've been weaned off the methadone, pronounced mentally healthy, and sent back to the front lines of the fourth grade. No matter that I was grotesquely disfigured, or that I was unable to sleep, or that I would fall to the floor crying like a little girl in the lightest summer drizzle.

Post-Traumatic Stress Disorder still wasn't listed in the Diagnostic and Statistical Manual of Mental Disorders in the mid-1970s. The profession of psychiatry was barely past the days of electroshock therapy and lobotomies. Besides, I was a kid, and kids are supposed to heal.

Dr. Kenny knew better.

Once I was pronounced drug free, he suggested we continue our sessions, "Just to talk." My parents agreed.

Dr. Kenny never mentioned the storm or my injuries in those first few years, and neither did I. He never made me recount the day of the lightning strike, never made me tell him about the hospital stays, and never asked me about the kids who'd tied me up.

When my parents and the police tried to get me to identify the little cretins that had done this to me, I pretended not to remember. But I did remember. Of course I remembered. I didn't tell anyone because I was scared shitless of those kids.

The funny thing is, I think those kids were more afraid of me than I was of them. They wouldn't look at me or talk to me. They wouldn't even pass by my house without first crossing the street. I guess they knew what they had done, and it kind of haunted them. You'd think that would've made me feel better, but really, it didn't.

Anyway, like I said, Dr. Kenny never asked me about any of that stuff. He didn't need to. Somehow he always managed to steer our sessions back to my relationships with other children, my feelings about fire, or worse, lightning.

"I don't like it," I told him, withdrawing into myself.

"Why not?"

"Because, it's stupid?"

"Why is lightning stupid?"

"Because it's dumb!"

"Why is it dumb?" Ask a nine-year-old a series of uninterrupted questions, and eventually you can steer the conversation anywhere you want. Try it some time.

"I dunno, because it hurts people."

"Okay then, Harry," he said, "the best way to avoid getting hurt by something is to understand it."

Dr. Kenny and I spent the next five sessions learning everything we could about lightning—from how a lightning bolt can be hotter than the surface of the sun, to how clouds turn into huge capacitors during electrical storms, to what a capacitor actually is. Whether he meant to or not—and I'm pretty sure he meant to—Dr. Kenny set in motion a lifelong pattern of learning for me. Analysis, logic, and calculation became my defense mechanisms against the world. I trained myself—strike that, Dr. Kenny trained me—to find comfort in tearing a thing down to its basic elements and building it back up in a way that I could understand. When things got really bad, I could wrap myself in a security blanket of cold, hard facts.

In the last of those five sessions, Dr. Kenny showed me a chart he'd found in a library book. It was a list of every kind of lightning known to man. I can still picture it clearly to this day.

"Harry," he said, "do you think you can remember this

list?" He saw me look confused, so he continued. "A lot of grown-ups use little tricks to help calm themselves down when they're upset, or when they're sad or frightened. Sometimes they'll count to ten, sometimes they'll try to remember the lyrics to a song. They use lists so they'll be distracted from whatever is bothering them."

"That works?" Dr. Kenny could see I wasn't really buying it.

"Just try it."

I did:

Intracloud Lightning
Cloud-to-Cloud Lightning
Cloud-to-Ground Lightning
Cloud-to-Air Lightning
Bolts from the Blue
Anvil Lightning
Ball Lightning
Bead Lightning
Forked Lightning
Heat Lightning
Ribbon Lightning
Streak Lightning
Triggered Lightning

It worked. I couldn't believe it, but it worked. The list became a kind of incantation for me. Anytime I was upset or scared, I would repeat it in my head over and over again until I calmed down.

Intracloud Lightning

Cloud-to-Cloud Lightning

Cloud-to-Ground Lightning

Cloud-to-Air Lightning

Bolts from the Blue

Anvil Lightning

Ball Lightning

Bead Lightning

Forked Lightning

Heat Lightning

Ribbon Lightning

Streak Lightning

Triggered Lightning

The Lightning List was the first of hundreds of lists that I've memorized over the years. They're like a slap in the face when anxiety hits. No strike that, not a slap in the face. They're like a reset button, like the ones they have at bowling alleys. The lists somehow manage to jolt my brain from being a jumbled mess and back into a functioning state.

Dr. Kenny was my Obi-Wan Kenobi, and my sessions with him were the best fifty minutes of my life each week. Sad but true.

As for those other doctors, the ones trying to fix my

flesh and bones, well, let's just say those visits didn't go quite as well. After five years of intense treatment, I was, and there's no other way to put it, a monster: splotches of discolored skin were mottled across my thirteen-year-old face and neck. Thick, pink ridgelines ran from my right temple to the base of the flattened snout that was my nose. Crinkly flesh replaced my eyebrows and eyelashes, giving me the look of a startled albino. It was all capped off by an obvious and unrealistic wig hiding spotty patches of hair, some of it black, some of it gray like dust. The sum total of my appearance formed the contour map of a strange world where even I wasn't welcome.

Between the war crime that was my face and the absences for doctors' visits, I was a ghost to the other kids at school, the boogeyman. No one knew what to make of me. The kids who were more or less nice—the ones who did their homework, played the clarinet or flute, and ate peanut butter and jelly sandwiches for lunch—left me alone.

The other kids did not.

WAITING ON A FRIEND

*(written by Mick Jagger and Keith Richards,
and performed by The Rolling Stones)*

I was sitting outside of Henry David Thoreau Middle School, eating my peanut butter and jelly sandwich, when a behemoth of a seventh grader—who could've passed for an eighteen-year-old, with facial hair, a husky voice, and a vague scent of aftershave—sat down next to me. He started rummaging through my lunch bag.

"Juice, banana . . . here we go, cupcake." He took the cupcake and smiled at me. I could hear his friends, a group of devoted henchman standing outside my field of vision, laughing and snorting. Bruised noses, bruised ribs, and a bruised ego taught me the only safe response: pretend it's not happening. I started to think my way through the New York Mets active roster: *John Stearns, Dave Kingman, Doug Flynn.*

The behemoth stood to go. "Thanks, freak."

Hubie Brooks, Frank Taveras, Mookie Wilson.

"I said thanks, freak," a bit more emphasis the second time. "I said . . ."

"That's enough, Billy. Give it back." It was a new voice, coming from somewhere behind me. I stopped my list and turned around.

A kid half Billy's size, even smaller than me, was standing there with his hands on his hips. His posture, while not exactly threatening, left no room to question his intentions.

Billy looked at me, looked at the new kid, and then back at me. "Whatever. I was just foolin' 'round anyways." He tossed the cupcake in the air—landing it in the outstretched hand of my benefactor—and walked away.

"Don't mind him," the new kid said. "He's harmless. I'm Johnny." I was so caught off guard that it took me a beat to register his other hand, the one not holding a cupcake, stretched in my direction. I shook it.

"I'm Harry Jones."

One of the more interesting exercises Dr. Kenny had me go through was the creation of something he called a *People Catalog*. "How do you see the rest of the world, Harry?" he'd asked. "How would you describe other people?"

"Describe them?"

"Find things they have in common, and put them into groups. You know, kids who are into sports, or adults who yell too much. That sort of thing."

Naturally, I built that catalog around my scars and

24

how other people saw them. I'm guessing that's what Dr. Kenny wanted:

Potsies. Named for the hangdog character from *Happy Days*, a Potsie can't figure out if he's supposed to look at me or look away. For a long time I thought this was pity. It's not. It's shame and guilt at being normal, in not having to bear my burden. It's why people look at the ground when they see someone with Down's syndrome, or a homeless person, or a kid with palsy. At some subconscious level most of you think that *you*—because of some horrible thing you've done, will do, or want to do—deserve a more sinister fate than me.

Nazis. A few people, like Billy the Behemoth, stare at my face, focusing on my scars. They see opportunity in my deformity, something to exploit and control. What they're really doing is responding to a Darwinian urge awakened at the genetic level, its goal to weed out evolution's mistakes. They're trying to purify the race.

Faints. The name is shorthand for "Faux Saints." This is the "holier than thou" crowd who want desperately to live on the moral high ground. They try to prove they have no prejudice by locking their gaze to mine, when in fact their discomfort is written in the stillness of their eyes: *See Harry, I'm treating you normally . . . I'm not staring at your scars at all.*

Freaks. There's a small group that likes to sneak furtive glances at my face, imagining, I suspect, a long tale involving muggers, terrorists, or pirates. It's like they get a boner at the thought of what I've been through. (Seriously, this happens.)

Friends. Then there's the truly rare breed, like Johnny McKenna, who don't seem to see the scars at all.

Thoreau was a two-year middle school, and with nearly three hundred and fifty kids in eighth grade alone, it was impossible to know everyone, so Johnny was a stranger to me. He had curly blond locks spilling over his forehead and framing a pair of ocean-colored eyes. And it was those eyes you noticed first. They commanded attention. No wait, they *demanded* attention. They were why I remained glued to the spot even though every fiber of my being was telling me to run.

Johnny sat down and we started talking. Strike that, *he* started talking. I didn't say two words. I was so unresponsive that I must've seemed weird or at least ungrateful, and I wondered why he didn't just walk away. Maybe he figured I was still reeling from the whole thing with the cupcake. Whatever the reason, Johnny stayed.

He talked about his brother Russell—"he's eighteen and he's super cool. He has an old Mustang that he lets me drive in the Caldor's parking lot, and a huge record collection he lets me listen to." He talked about his parents—"my dad's a chemical engineer and my mom teaches classics at Concordia. They're mostly okay, ya know, for parents." He talked about how he ran three miles every night before dinner—"I'm going to go out for track next year in high school. I want to run in the New York City Marathon some day." And he described in detail, often quoting from, the music and comic books and television shows that formed the axis on which his world seemed to revolve—"Nanu Nanu, Harry!"

The more he talked, the more I let my guard down. I wasn't even aware at first that I'd started talking back.

"I collect baseball cards. I have every complete Topps set from 1973 forward. The best part is—" I heard the sound of my own voice and stopped. Talking to other kids was anathema to me. (Please note, FAP, the great use of an SAT word—*anathema*—in context, in spite of what I'm sure you think are my lackluster SAT scores.) Anyway, hearing my own voice was like walking onto a frozen lake in early spring, knowing the ice was going to collapse beneath my feet any second.

But Johnny just sat there, smiling. It was a patient smile, like watching a cat blink. It made me want to blink back. Before long I was telling him how I was almost struck by lightning. When the bell rang we went our separate ways and I didn't see Johnny again that afternoon.

The next day during recess, Johnny was at the center of a group of boys, the lot of them orbiting around his

Reaganesque charm and hanging on his every word. I sat down alone nearby. I'd just started on that day's peanut butter and jelly sandwich when Johnny called me over.

"Hey Harry, c'mere."

Everything froze.

I felt a rush of vertigo as I stood up. A narrow aisle parted through the throng of kids around Johnny. They were like menacing trees come to life, making an eerie path through a dense and uninviting wood. The tension pulled what was left of my skin tauter than usual as I felt them stare at me—*the weird kid with the scars, what's he doing here?* When I reached the center of the swarm, Johnny said, "Hey, do you guys know Harry Jones? He was struck by lightning!" I held my breath, thinking I'd been duped into some new and twisted form of torture. I noticed the other kids looking at Johnny, waiting for a cue. Johnny noticed, too.

He shifted down the bench on which he was perched, motioning with a nod of his head for me to join him. Time, which had stopped, started ticking forward again.

"That's neat," one of the other kids said to me. "I mean, not *neat*, but wow! Did it hurt?"

And just like that, I was accepted. I was cool by association. For the first time in my life, I was starting to fit in.

OUR HOUSE

(written by Michael Barson, Mark William Bedford, Christopher John Foreman, Graham McPherson, Charles Smyth, Lee Jay Thompson, and Daniel Woodgate, and performed by Madness)

After Billy the Behemoth "introduced" us, Johnny and I started spending a lot of time together. I don't think there's any explanation for how people become friends. Maybe it's pheromones (we learned about pheromones in tenth grade biology), maybe it's kismet (we learned about kismet in eleventh grade English), or maybe there's no reason or explanation at all (I learned about unexplained things from Leonard Nimoy's *In Search Of* TV series). With kids, there's an even greater intensity to the speed at which new friendships form. To me, it seems like magic.

I'd show up at Johnny's house most nights to join him on his training runs. His mother hated that I was there. She'd put on her best smile and speak to me in a loud and slow voice, like I was retarded, deaf, or both.

"Well, hello Harry. And how are you today?"

She and Johnny's dad, Mr. McKenna—to this day I still don't know either of their first names—must've figured that I was their son's charity case, that I was there because he took pity on me. The more often I turned up, the less friendly they became. Johnny didn't seem to notice, and if he didn't notice, I didn't care. It was a small price to pay for the pleasure of his company.

I could never quite keep up with Johnny when we ran. He would slow his pace just enough to let me almost catch up, and when I got too close, he'd put on the jets and pull away. That's just who he was.

When he had run his allotted distance he would flop down on some neighbor's lawn panting and laughing and I'd follow suit.

"What are you doing for Halloween?" he asked me out of the blue one night.

Since the lightning strike, I'd made a point of avoiding Halloween. It was my least favorite night of the year. Other kids would transform themselves into the monster I already was, going from door to door scaring people into giving them treats. That I didn't need a costume was a miserable reminder of everything I hated about life.

"I'm not really into Halloween," I told him.

"Come to my house," he said, ignoring my answer. "We're going to have fun."

I shook my head no and changed the subject.

"My parents," I told him, "want to meet you."

You have to understand, for five solid years, since 1976 to be exact, I only left the house to go to school, doctors' appointments, or wherever else I was dragged. That I was suddenly leaving of my own accord was a shock to my parents' system. They didn't know whether to open a bottle of champagne or call an exorcist. They took the middle ground and invited Johnny to dinner.

It was a few days before Halloween when Johnny showed up at my house. When I answered the door he was wearing a sport jacket and carrying flowers. Johnny was strictly a jeans and T-shirt kid, so at first I wasn't even sure who I was looking at.

"Aren't you going to invite me in, Harry?" he asked.

"Yes, yes," my mom said from behind me, "invite him in."

I was too stunned to say anything, so I just stepped aside and let Johnny pass.

"Mrs. Jones," Johnny said, "these are for you." He held the flowers out, and I swear my mother almost cried when she took them.

"Mr. Jones," Johnny continued, approaching my dad, who was standing just behind my mom, slack-jawed and dumbfounded, "it's nice to meet you, sir." *Sir?* Johnny held out his hand and my dad took it. "I'm Johnny McKenna. Thank you for inviting me over."

It turns out I wasn't the only one who didn't know how to relate to kids my age. My parents were just as clueless.

My mom hadn't worked since the lightning strike.

Her life, post-storm, as I think I've already told you, was defined entirely by me. It was my dad who was the bread-winner. He was a political campaign consultant, work-ing mostly on statewide elections. For a man who loved to argue as much as my dad did, it was the right kind of work. Most nights over dinner, he would introduce a topic that would get the three of us debating. Sometimes it was serious stuff like "What happens when the world runs out of oil?" Sometimes it was light stuff like "Who's funnier, Lenny or Squiggy?"

But on the night Johnny came over, my dad, for the first time I could remember, seemed flummoxed. When you stop to think about it, it kind of makes sense.

If I'd had a normal childhood, my parents would have been broken-in by a steady diet of increasingly older and more sophisticated friends. Instead, they skipped over all that and got right to Johnny. It was like having your first driving lesson. On the interstate. During rush hour.

Johnny took the seat my dad offered and proceeded to give my parents his entire life story. I didn't join the conversation. Not because I was freaked out or nervous, but because there was no natural opening. Johnny and my parents, mostly my dad, basked in the warm glow of each other's company. I was something of an ornament.

That made me feel good and bad at the same time, but it didn't really matter. More than anything I was proud and happy to show my parents that I wasn't a total freak, at least not anymore. Not only did I have a friend, I had *this* friend.

My mom shot me the occasional look throughout the night, making sure I was doing okay, like she always did.

I'd actually started to zone out when something Johnny was saying caught my attention.

". . . excited that Harry's going to be joining us for trick-or-treating on Halloween."

What? Did he just say I'm going trick-or-treating?

My parents, who were well versed in my views on Halloween—mostly from my annual October 31 sob fest—looked at each other and then at me, and then back at each other. After a beat, they both started talking at once, falling over each other at how happy they were to hear the news.

"Wonderful," said my mom.

"Best thing for him," my dad said to Johnny like I wasn't even there.

When the celebration subsided, all three of them looked at me.

"Great," I said weakly. Johnny's face was all smirk.

After dinner was over, after Johnny helped clear and wash the dishes, after the four of us watched *Laverne and Shirley* together, it was time for Johnny to go home.

As I watched both my parents hug him goodnight, I have to admit that I felt a pang of jealousy. *This is what it must feel like to be normal,* I thought.

I walked out of the house with Johnny. As soon as the front door closed behind us, he gave me a high five.

"Awesome, Harry," he said. "Trust me, they're going to let you stay out as long as you want on Halloween." He walked down the street toward his house, adding, "See you at school tomorrow" as he went.

Halloween. I had told Johnny "no" about Halloween because I really wanted to stay home. The thought of being out with other kids made me physically nauseous. But thanks to his stunt with my parents, I was trapped.

When I look back now, I see that this was the beginning of what would become a well-established pattern of Johnny deciding and me doing.

As I went back up the steps to my house I overheard my parents' muffled voices on the other side of the door.

"What a fine young man," my father was saying.

"I'll say," my mother offered. "The two of them are lucky to have found one another."

"The two of them?" my dad answered. "Let's call a spade a spade, Ruth, Harry's the lucky one here."

"Ben, hush, he'll hear you."

I waited another minute until I heard them take their conversation into the kitchen, and snuck back inside. I pretended not to have heard anything, said goodnight, and went straight to bed.

HELLO, I LOVE YOU

(written by John Densmore, Robby Krieger, Ray Manzarek, and Jim Morrison, and performed by The Doors)

I arrived at Johnny's house on Halloween night 1981 decked out in my dad's tattered cotton trousers, faded button-down shirt, threadbare suit jacket, and old fedora. I was sporting the costume of choice for discriminating suburbanite teens: I was a bum. I'd even burnt a piece of cork and smeared it all over my cheeks, nose, and chin.

Everyone was already outside when I got there. They were all dressed exactly like me and all holding pillowcase sacks filled with eggs and shaving cream, ready to battle each other, mailboxes, cars, or anything else that got in our way. We looked like a pack of short, skinny 1940s hobos.

I'd expected to find Johnny and a few boys I knew from school. Instead, it was Johnny and a whole lot of kids I didn't know, including a bunch of girls from the Our Lady of the Perpetual Who-Can-Remember-the-Name Catholic School.

Girls.

Catholic school girls!

"Harry, I want you to meet someone."

I froze.

"This is Gabrielle Privat."

My tongue tied itself in a neat little knot and a bowling ball dropped from my esophagus to my stomach. My fingertips and toes went numb.

"Harry?" Johnny asked. I finally managed to mutter a sheepish hello back, though I said it more to my shoes than to Gabrielle's face.

Right from the start, I was smitten with Gabrielle. I was a gargoyle around girls on a good day; hideous, mute, and petrified. And this wasn't a girl, this was a goddess. She was my age, and even with her own smudged face and porkpie hat, I could see she was beautiful. The softness of her skin, the delicacy of her features shone through the smeared ash. The way I remembered it later, she was glowing, *literally* glowing. I'm surprised I didn't pass out. I secretly cursed Johnny for turning the night into a disaster before it began.

But that's the funny thing. It wasn't a disaster at all. It was one of the best nights of my life.

For reasons I've never fully understood, I stepped outside of myself that night. I was possessed by some holy spirit, speaking in tongues and walking on water. I was my wittiest, funniest, and most charming self. Maybe the burnt-cork-soot on my face was a mask, a safe place to hide, a place from which I could finally venture forth. But I think the real reason was Gabrielle.

She and I spent most of the night talking and laughing. We covered every topic held sacrosanct (SAT word alert!) by white, middle-class thirteen-year-olds: Our favorite TV shows, like *Taxi* and *WKRP*; the classes in school we didn't totally hate, like English or history; and MTV, the newest, coolest thing either one of us had ever seen. We ignored our solemn egging responsibilities and existed outside the group, outside the world. We were lost in the sphere of each other.

Our friends, boys and girls both, recognized what was going on, and other than the occasional squirt of Barbasol on the back of my head, left us alone.

As the night drew to a close, Gabrielle and I offered each other a nervous half-wave, our faces ready to crack from suppressed smiles. I headed home with no candy and with no mischief accomplished, but with a strange and wonderful fluttering in my heart.

When I visited Johnny the next day—the visit a pretense to see Gabrielle—it, of course, all came crashing down.

She was disappointed to see me in the light of day. With no soot on my face or hat on my head, my disfigured skin was revealed in all its gruesome glory. And with my mask gone, I reverted back to my shy, awkward self. We spent a few uncomfortable minutes chatting before she made a weak excuse and left. Johnny walked her to the door.

I didn't need to read between the lines of Johnny's white lie—about Gabrielle not being allowed to date, about how sorry she was—to know the truth. She saw the real me, a scarred little boy, scarred on the outside and scarred on the inside. She turned tail and ran.

I would learn later, on a class trip to the Bronx Botanical Garden, that Gabrielle Privat was the name of a species of rose. Its flower had a delicate, fleeting beauty, its attraction one of form over substance. I guess that sounds kind of petty, but hey, it's the truth.

Anyway, I must've folded myself up like an envelope, sealed with no way in or out, because the next thing Johnny said was, "We should start a band."

It was a strange thing to say. He could've said, "Don't worry, there will be lots of other girls," or "Let's go listen to some records," or "How about we walk down the hill and get some ice cream." But no, he said, "We should start a band."

I could only guess he was trying to distract me, trying to stop me from falling down a well of self-pity and self-doubt. It was either an act of kindness or sympathy or both. Whatever it was, I should've just walked away. But Johnny was Johnny. He had a knack for knowing the right thing to say, the right joke to tell, the right expression to wear on his face at just the right moment.

Neither one of us had ever touched an instrument or knew the first thing about playing music, and none of this was going to erase Gabrielle—even time, healer of all healers would do a half-assed job with that one.

The only thing I could think to say was, "Sure, let's start a band."

And *that* was how it all began.

DAYDREAM BELIEVER

(written by John C. Stewart, and performed by The Monkees)

That same afternoon, the day Johnny had suggested the idea of a band to soothe my dented ego, we were lying on his bedroom floor, daydreaming and planning our meteoric rise to superstardom. We were at an age when kids were starting to identify themselves by the music they listened to: there were the headbangers and clubbers, the rockers and punks, even the Broadway musical wannabes. And then there was us, determined to defy definition.

Johnny's older brother Russell had a collection of albums spanning thirty years and we devoured every disc, every track, every groove. We started with the Beatles (*Help!* and *Rubber Soul* all the way through *The White Album* and *Abbey Road*), graduated to *Exile on Main Street*, *Physical Graffiti*, and *Quadrophenia* (the greatest album ever recorded), and did our postdoctoral work with Elvis Costello, Richard Hell, and the Clash. We sampled Miles Davis and John Coltrane. We even dabbled in Johnny Cash and Merle Haggard. Nothing eluded our grasp.

Every day we spent hours and hours watching those black discs spin, listening to the pop and hiss of the needle riding the imperfections in the vinyl until the first chords took over. We'd lie on our stomachs poring over every inch of the album cover, the back album cover, the liner notes, and, if we were lucky enough to have them, the lyrics.

As we lay there that day, a new record from a band called Black Flag was on the turntable. If the Sex Pistols made the Who and Led Zeppelin sound like they were singing anthems from another age, Black Flag made the Sex Pistols seem overproduced and corporate, if that's even possible. This was a bunch of guys with a guitar, a bass, and a drum set that were—or at least it sounded like they were—recording in someone's living room. And they sounded drunk. (While I didn't have any frame of reference for knowing what a drunk band would sound like, I was pretty sure this was it.) Songs like "Six Pack," "TV Party," and "Gimme Gimme Gimme" stitched themselves into a kind of manifesto for Johnny and me.

These guys really didn't care what anyone else thought. It's like they were giving the world the finger, and they thought it was really, really funny. We did, too. The entire album, from the first note to the last, infused our conversation with energy and excitement.

Johnny, as usual, did most of the talking. He would be the lead singer. I would play guitar. We'd find a drummer and a bass player, and maybe a second guitar player. We'd write our own songs because nobody cool ever did cover tunes. We'd have "gigs" (a new word for me that day) at clubs in the Village, and we'd drink beers, and we'd go on tour, and we'd meet girls, and we'd get laid. (Not a new word.)

I just listened, letting the daydream wash over me, cleansing Gabrielle from the surface, letting her sink to a deeper place where she could live in my memory to teach and occasionally haunt me.

"What should we call ourselves?" Johnny asked the question more to himself than to me. I'd hardly said two words as he laid out his vision for the band, so I surprised us both when I spoke.

"How about the Scar Boys?"

For a moment, Johnny was startled. Then he smiled wider than the Grand Canyon. "Brilliant, Harry. Fucking brilliant!"

When I woke the next morning, a rain-soaked Monday, the memory of that afternoon seemed real but insubstantial, like steam. I knew all that stuff about starting a band would be forgotten as quickly as it had been said, that its purpose was to make me forget about Halloween, to ease the blow of getting dumped before ever having had a girlfriend. But when I caught up with Johnny at school, he was standing at his locker with a seventh grader I recognized but didn't know. "Harry, meet Richie, the Scar Boys' drummer."

Richie, whose unruly chestnut hair made him seem every bit of his five foot ten inch frame and then some, let out a whoop and high-fived me. My jaw must have gone slack (something physical therapy had helped me learn how to do), because the two of them just stood there laughing.

Later that day, Johnny, who worked the school like he was running for office, found our bass player. A quiet kid from period seven social studies, Dave spent most of the class creating intricate drawings of birds, planes, or trees blowing in the wind on the margins of his spiral notebook.

In rounding up bandmates, Johnny had also committed us to play three different holiday parties in late December. There was no turning back.

ROCK AND ROLL BAND

(written by Tom Scholz, and performed by Boston)

My parents, even five years later, wore the incident of the thunderstorm like a Scarlet A. Their guilt at finding me tied to that tree half alive—as if they could've controlled or prevented it—hung over our house like summer smog. As time wore on I grew to resent it. It made me feel like I'd done something wrong, but it had its advantages, too.

When I told my mom I wanted to play guitar, the same day Johnny had introduced me to my new band-mates, she lit up like a Christmas tree. Before I knew what was happening, I was whisked to the local music store and outfitted with a new Fender Stratocaster, a Peavey amp, and a schedule of lessons once a week from Rick, the long-haired, tattooed "dude" who ran the guitar department.

Rick played lead guitar in a sixties tribute band called

the Skittish Invasion. Their set list covered everything from Gerry and the Pacemakers to Jimi Hendrix, and they appeared regularly at a handful of local bars.

"The money's decent, but the best part's the chicks." Rick talked to me like I was an equal. Strike that. He didn't talk to me like I was an equal at all. He was Kung Fu and I was Grasshopper. But he didn't talk to me like I was a freak. He made me believe it was my right to expect every success he'd found with the guitar. Of course, I didn't know at the time that the success he'd found was, well, kind of lame. Back then I thought Rick was a rock star, and I wanted to be just like him. I really did.

In the year and a half I spent taking lessons, Rick taught me basic music theory, gave me drills to make my pick-hand nimble, and showed me how to use a slide. Together we went to school on blues, rock, and country guitar styles, covering everything from pentatonic scales, to how to dampen the strings when using a distortion pedal without causing too much feedback. And, most important, he imbued me with the ancient and sacred knowledge that the most beautiful part of music is the space between the notes.

I don't think I can ever repay Rick for giving me the gift of music. It is the single greatest gift I've ever received. Praise the lord and amen.

But all that took time.

When I arrived at the Scar Boys' first rehearsal, a mere

four weeks and four guitar lessons later, I'd only managed to learn three chords—A, D, and G. Through relentless hours of practice, groping the Braille of the fret board, I'd trained my hand to creep from one chord to the other and back again. As Johnny, Richie, Dave, and I stood there, staring at each other like a bunch of Neanderthals trying to figure out how to make a fire, I started to play.

A to D, A to D, A to D to G. A to D, A to D, A to D to G.

Dave, who had even less musical experience than me, asked what I was playing, so I shouted out each chord as I strummed it, and he managed to find the matching note on his bass.

A to D, A to D, A to D to G. A to D, A to D, A to D to G.

Richie, who had even less musical experience than Dave, found what little rhythm we were cobbling together and added a flailing but rudimentary four-four beat.

Tick tick tap tap. Tick tick tap tap. Tick tick tap tap.

Johnny grabbed his old Invicta cassette recorder, pressed the "play" and "record" buttons together, and started to sing. I can't remember the words now, but I think it was called "Middle Class Blues." It was a song about the drudgery of doing chores and the ills of author-ity, an anthem for teenage angst. When I listen to that tape now, I'm surprised at how earsplittingly, dog-howl-ingly awful we were. But when you're thirteen and you can string three chords together in any organized way, to your own ears you're the Beatles.

A few weeks later we played four original songs at each of those three holiday parties. Maybe no one had the heart to tell us we stank, or maybe they saw the chemistry and the potential of the Scar Boys and wanted to egg us on. Whatever the reason, they loved us. Or so the other guys told me.

Being onstage, having a spotlight shining on me, even metaphorically, was terrifying. I was still the misfit, still the monster. I played each of those gigs with my dad's fedora (the one from Halloween) pulled low over my face, a pair of dark sunglasses, and a denim jacket with the collar turned up, and I spent most of the time facing Richie, with my back to the audience. Johnny tried to convince me that the name of the band would make a lot more sense if I could let my guard down, show my face. But I wasn't ready. After a while he backed off and stopped asking.

We played on like this through ninth and tenth grades, making occasional appearances at friends' parties, but mostly just jamming in my parents' basement.

When we weren't playing music, Johnny and I spent every free minute together. We'd lie on the grass hill by the elementary school, spotting animals, cars, and musical instruments in the clouds during the day, and counting stars at night. We'd leave empty soda cans, and pennies, and once even a history textbook, on the commuter rail tracks, watching the ten-car train demolish whatever was in its path. We'd cut school and sneak in through the movie theater's back door to see *Return of the Jedi,* or *War Games,* or

The Right Stuff. We'd try to work up the nerve to talk to girls at the mall, Johnny so effortlessly succeeding, me staying back, lurking in the shadows like the Phantom of the Opera.

And, of course, I'd join Johnny on his nightly run.

It was this last thing, the evening run, that was my favorite ritual. While I didn't have the same soul-infusing love of running that Johnny did, I saw the appeal. It was easy to lose yourself in the sound of shoes slapping on the pavement, in the whoosh of wind in your ears. It felt good to be moving. Whether we were running away from something or toward something I didn't know, and I didn't care.

My friendship with Johnny was making everything better. Even school was becoming bearable. I was still one rung lower on the social ladder than Tina, the girl who'd crapped her pants in the second grade (there are some things you can never live down; her family probably should have moved after that happened), and two rungs lower than Lance, our school's one and only deaf kid, but classmates who used to laugh at me would now at least nod in my direction, and a small but growing group of kids—mostly the ones that circled Johnny—were becoming my friends.

And then, when we hit the eleventh grade, something strange happened. Something no one anticipated or could have predicted. The Scar Boys got good.

SCHOOL'S OUT

(written by Michael O. Bruce, Glen Buxton, Alice Cooper,
Dennis Dunaway, and Neal A. Smith, and performed by Alice Cooper)

It was around this time that my grades hit rock bottom and my parents were called to the school for a meeting with the principal.

Mom and Dad got there a few minutes early, and the three of us sat in the seats outside the principal's office in uncomfortable silence. That this meeting had been called wasn't a surprise to anyone.

The first few years after the lightning strike, when I was spending more time in hospital beds than classrooms, I was never able to catch up in school. The best I could manage was to squeak by. It's not that I wasn't smart enough, it's that I was too physically and emotionally tired to do the work. My parents tried hiring tutors, but there just wasn't enough gas in my tank for academics.

Even after I stopped the doctors' visits and even after

I started to live a more normal life—thanks in large part to Johnny—I never became the kind of student my parents hoped I would be.

"You know, Harry," my father would tell me each time he saw my report card, "a boy like you will have few prospects in life if he doesn't go to a good college." I didn't know if a "boy like me" was a boy who *looked* like me or a boy who *tested* like me. I'm not sure which one was worse.

My dad, who didn't look pleased to be sitting outside the principal's office, was just raising his finger to say something when the door opened and we were called inside.

"Mr. and Mrs. Jones, Harry, please come in," the secretary said. She closed the door behind us as we entered.

The principal, Mr. Sewicky, was a thick, lurching man who wore suits that were too small; it always seemed like he was going to bust out of his clothes like the Hulk. His hair was cut short in a military style, and on his desk was a gold-colored golf ball affixed to a piece of wood with a plaque that read "Hole in One, Stillwater Greens, October 1978." Behind him on the wall was a mounted and stuffed fish that didn't look happy. Why Mr. Sewicky was a principal in suburban New York instead of, say, Oklahoma, is a mystery to me.

He didn't come out from behind his desk to shake anyone's hand. Instead, he motioned to three empty seats and we all sat down.

This was the first time my parents had ever been called to Mr. Sewicky's office. Not so for me. The principal and I had become well acquainted over the years. While I had been called down once or twice to talk about grades, more often it was because one or more of the school's thugs had been picking on me.

Even though I had started to make friends, and even though hanging around a popular kid like Johnny McKenna offered a certain level of protection, that protection had its limits. I was still a favorite target of the school's Nazi youth. There was no shortage of kids like Billy the Behemoth in high school, and I was one of their go-to guys.

There were the obvious things like wedgies and punches and kicks, but sometimes the more twisted of the school's goons would get creative. There was a kind of art to it.

The worst was in ninth grade shop class when a boy named Alvaro Dimatteo discovered the mystery and wonders of a blowtorch. (You need a license to drive a car or own a gun, but the board of education will hand any fourteen- or fifteen-year-old a blowtorch. I need someone to explain that to me.)

I don't know if Alvaro knew about my deeply ingrained fear of fire, but it didn't matter. Five minutes into class he had me pinned into a corner, the lit blowtorch a few inches from my arms, which were held cowering over my head. When the teacher pulled him off and sent us both to the principal's office, the other students cheered. They weren't cheering for me.

Mr. Sewicky went through the motions of scolding Alvaro, but you could tell his heart wasn't in it. There was an unspoken understanding between the two of them: Alvaro had only done what nature had commanded him to do. He could no more help beating on me than a hawk could stop itself from scooping up a mouse. By the end of the session, the principal was telling me that I should do less to provoke other children.

As soon as he sent us on our way and we were in the hall, Alvaro shoved me hard into a row of lockers, laughed, and moved on. I never told anyone about that incident, not Johnny, not Dr. Kenny, not my parents. That's just how things were.

"I think we all know why we're here," Mr. Sewicky said to my parents. "Harry, his difficulties notwithstanding"—the word *difficulties* stuck in his teeth like a piece of uncooked popcorn—"is failing two of his classes, and is getting a C in two of the others. The only bright spot seems to be arithmetic."

I snuck a peek at my father. If he clenched his jaw any harder, he was going to need to see a dentist.

"His teachers seem to think he has more potential than that." From the tone of his voice, it was pretty clear that Mr. Sewicky didn't agree with them.

"We're very sorry, Mr. Sewicky," my father offered. His tone of voice suggested that he and the principal were both Men and that their Manliness gave them an intuitive understanding of the situation. "Isn't that right, Harry?" my father asked.

I nodded.

"Harry," my father said to me, "how much of this has to do with your little musical group?" (And yes, he actually said "little musical group.")

"Oh, Ben, no," my mother interjected. "That band is so good for Harry."

Both Mr. Sewicky and my father looked at my mother like she had just parachuted in from a Russian Mig. Her cheeks flushed, she turned her head, and she looked out the window.

"I know about this band," Mr. Sewicky said. "Johnny McKenna's in it."

I nodded again.

"Tell me, Harry," he said, "how come Johnny's grades aren't slipping?"

The answer, of course, had nothing to do with music. It was because Johnny cared and I didn't. But that didn't seem like a smart thing to say, so I just shrugged my shoulders.

"Harry's grades have slipped low enough," Mr. Sewicky said to my dad, "that if he can't turn things around, I'm going to be forced to consider academic probation."

I didn't really know what "academic probation" was, but I'd seen *Animal House* and all I could think of was Dean Wormer putting the Deltas on "double secret probation" and a small, barely noticeable chuckle escaped from my lips.

I say *barely* noticeable because Mr. Sewicky asked, "Are you finding this funny, Harry?"

"No, sir," I said, and put my head down. That was kind of a lie. I thought it was funny for three reasons:

Reason #1: If you take a step back, the whole situation was kind of ridiculous. It's like adults think that tackling problems at the surface equals tackling *problems*. It doesn't. If they wanted me to do better at school, they probably should've been talking about why I hated the place so much, why I was terrified to set foot in that school each and every day. They should have been talking about Billy the Behemoth and Alvaro Dimatteo.

Reason #2: I couldn't help staring at that mounted fish. I was sure it was watching me and I was sure it was smiling. No, I wasn't taking any drugs, prescribed or otherwise. I guess I was bored enough by the whole situation that my imagination was getting the better of me.

Reason #3: I'd already given up on school. Playing guitar was all I wanted to do. None of what anyone was saying really mattered at all. And when nothing matters, it's kind of funny.

Don't get me wrong, I was smart enough to know that I had to pull my grades up at least a little bit, and I did. My parents weren't going to tolerate a high school dropout living under their roof, so appearances mattered. I would play along, but only as much as I needed to.

My father and the principal talked some more, I nodded and said yes some more, and everyone left thinking it was mission accomplished. I knew better.

Later that night, when I was in my room listening to Elvis Costello's *Trust* with the headphones on, someone opened the door.

It was my mom. She didn't say anything; she just walked in, put down a mint chocolate chip ice-cream sundae with an Oreo on top, kissed me on the head, and left. That was the thing about my mom, she was always on my side. Yeah, she wanted me to do better in school, and yeah, she worried about my future every bit as much as my dad. But at the end of the day what she really wanted was for me to be happy.

No matter how much was wrong with the world, that, at least, would always be right.

DAVE

(written by Bob Geldof, and performed by the Boomtown Rats)

The Scar Boys' first real gig was in the fall of 1984 at the world-famous CBGB's on the Bowery in New York City.

Ronald Reagan and Walter Mondale were trading barbs in a series of what seemed like staged presidential debates that October, and the whole country seemed to be getting meaner. There were few places for social misfits like me to retreat from the exclamations of "Where's the Beef" and "Go ahead, make my day." CBGB's was one of them.

Every Monday the club held what it called a "showcase night." If they liked your demo tape enough, they let you play for free. If you brought enough of your friends through the door, they gave you a paying gig on a better night. CB's got free live entertainment, and every band in New York got a shot.

Carol, the booking agent for CB's, "loved" our demo

tape. At least that's what Johnny told us. We were going to be the second of six bands on the bill and we'd have half an hour, exactly enough time to play all seven of our original songs.

From the moment the gig was booked, we rehearsed nonstop. Every day after school we ran through each of those songs in my parents' basement. Then Johnny made us play them again. And again. And then again. We were determined and methodical, and it paid off. Richie, Dave, and I fused our instruments into a single, rhythmic buzz saw, while Johnny gave each song character and depth. We were becoming a well-oiled, punk-pop machine. The Scar Boys were going to blow the roof off CBGB's, all the way from the Bowery to the East River. And we would have, I swear to God in heaven we would have. If only Dave had shown up.

The afternoon of the showcase, Johnny, Richie, and I skipped school and wandered around the East Village. We went from one secondhand clothing shop to the next, trying on shirts with angry torn fabric, tight leather pants, and scaly maroon boots so pointy they could be classified as weapons. It was all a vain attempt to camouflage the fact that we were just a bunch of green kids from the suburbs.

I settled on an outfit of brown pants, a mauve smoking jacket, and a big burgundy hat with a floppy brim that would just about completely hide my face. I was planning to cap it all off with my trademark sunglasses. For some reason, I'd convinced myself that looking like a pimp would make me blend in. Go figure.

It didn't matter. Johnny was having none of it. He was pushing me to wear a pair of skintight, red denim pants, and a black shirt covered with zippers that had no apparent meaning or function.

"C'mon Harry, you can still wear the hat and sunglasses," he told me.

I really didn't want to call any more attention to myself than I had to, but you didn't say no to Johnny McKenna.

Johnny was the kind of kid who'd been overindulged by his parents. You know these kids. They're the little brats who hear daily how smart they are, how handsome, how strong, how fast, how funny, how kind, how considerate, how clever, how wise they are.

One group of these kids gets addicted to the attention, growing up to need constant approval and reassurance. They throw tantrums in public and excel at school. They get good grades, partly to please their parents and partly because they're such insufferable little jerkwads that they have no friends and nothing better to do with their time than study.

The other group of overindulged kids uses the coddling to gain confidence. They walk with a strident gait, laugh easily, and test well. Johnny fit squarely into this latter camp. (I was overindulged, too, but for different reasons, so neither stereotype described me. One more way not to fit in, I suppose.)

When Johnny showed me his own outfit for the gig—black shirt, black pants, black boots; Johnny Cash, simple, elegant, cool—I was annoyed.

"Why should I be the one wearing fire-engine red? You're the front man."

"It's just the opposite for me," he explained. "The singer is in the spotlight. He needs to be understated."

I looked to Richie for support, but he just shrugged his shoulders and wandered to the register to buy his own ensemble, a T-shirt with a bull's-eye at its center and a giant brass belt buckle in the shape of a ten-gallon hat. I was on my own.

Truth is, over those first few years of our friendship, I'd become something of a reluctant sycophant to Johnny, and it was getting harder and harder to break out of that role. While he was the main reason—maybe the only reason—I was becoming my own person, he also kept me in check. It was okay for me to come out of my shell, as long as I didn't come out too far. If you didn't let Johnny be the center of attention, he had no use for you. And even though I don't think I understood it then, I needed Johnny, and needed Johnny to need me.

I held the red pants and the black shirt in my hands

and looked at him. "I can still wear my sunglasses?"

"Yes."

"And my hat?"

"Sure," he said, smiling at me. Some part of Johnny, I suspect, liked that I was still cowed by my own shame. "I just think this combo will look cool onstage," he added.

I nodded and the deal was struck.

Sporting our new duds, Johnny, Richie, and I arrived at CB's at five-thirty for our six p.m. sound check, expecting to meet Dave, who, in his understated way, had mumbled something about taking the train and meeting us in the city. When it came our turn for the sound check, Dave was MIA, so we swapped slots with another band and soaked in our surroundings.

A long, narrow space with a bar on the right-hand wall and a stage at the far end, CBGB's oozed character. I'd been a few times before, but those visits were at night, when the lights were low and the room was shrouded in mystery. During the sound check, in the grim reality of overhead fluorescence, CB's was laid bare, a magician's trick revealed. I watched a pierced girl vacuum the battle-worn carpet, her face a mask of total apathy. I ran my fingers along the scoring on the rough-hewn tables, feeling the ruts left by knives, forks, safety pins, and fingernails. I smelled the decade of cigarette smoke and body odor caked on to the high ceiling. And I studied, with the intensity of a graduate student studying theoretical physics, the layer upon layer of bumper sticker, spray paint, and ink covering every exposed surface.

The mere thought that in just a few hours I'd be standing on the same stage that so many punk and rock icons had stood on before—Johnny Ramone and Lenny Kaye, Jerry Harrison and Chris Stein—almost made me cry. It was as if all my dreams had come true. *If there's a nightclub in heaven*, I thought, *it's going to be just like CBGB's.*

Beyond the stage were the dressing rooms, cramped spaces so covered with graffiti that no hint of the original walls was visible. You had the feeling that if someone were to clean the band names, sex jokes, and insults away, the entire place would collapse into dust, leaving a gaping hole on the Bowery.

A twenty-something guy tuning his guitar saw me admiring the wall and handed me a Magic Marker. I mumbled an inaudible and monosyllabic "thankyou" as I took it, and in small but confident letters added "The Scar Boys" to the litany of names that had come before.

I could hear the band finishing its sound check and went back out front. Still no sign of Dave. We gave the next slot to the next band in line and Johnny went to find a pay phone to call Dave's house. Richie and I, who never had much to say to each other, listened to the soundman get levels from the three-piece onstage.

"Okay, just the bass drum." Thud, thud, thud, thud.

"Good, now the mounted toms." Bong thwap, bong thwap, bong thwap.

"Great. Play the whole kit." The drummer, who couldn't hold a candle to Richie, put together a simple beat as the engineer tweaked the volume and EQ.

"He's not coming." Richie and I both jumped, more startled at the words Johnny shouted over the noise than at his sudden reappearance. He held a hand up to stop us from the barrage of questions he could see we were about to unleash.

"His mother didn't say why. He's home, he wouldn't come to the phone. He's not coming."

The music stopped mid-sentence, and Johnny found himself shouting the word "coming!" He said it a second time, "He's not coming," quiet and restrained.

I don't know if we sat there staring at each other and grinding our teeth for three seconds, three minutes, or three weeks. I do remember that, in that moment, I was more conscious than ever of my ridiculous bright-red pants.

Richie was the first to act. He shook his head, spat on the ground, and got up to leave. He knew what we all knew—we couldn't go on without a bass player, it just wouldn't work. We packed our equipment, made up a story for the girl at the door that a member of our band had been in a car accident, and left.

So ended the first, almost glorious gig of the Scar Boys.

When we tried to confront Dave the next day at school, he would only hang his head, whisper an apology, and tell us he was quitting the band. We pushed him pretty hard for an answer, but it was no use. Whatever Dave's reasons were, he was keeping them to himself. To this day I still don't know what happened. Maybe his parents stepped in, worried their son was about to piss his life away. Or maybe the thought of an actual gig, compared to a high school party, was too much for his wilting demeanor. Whatever the reason, after three years of almost constant companionship, Dave, just like that, was gone.

PUNK ROCK GIRL

*(written by Genaro, Linderman, Sabatino, and Schulthise,
and performed by the Dead Milkmen)*

Johnny wasted no time:

*"The Scar Boys are holding auditions for a new bass player
today after school at 55 Elberon Ave.* (That was my house.)
Bring your instrument and bring your chops."

The handwritten ads were plastered all over school the
day after the CBGB's debacle, and we were floored when
half a dozen kids showed up. Johnny had them wait in the
backyard, calling each one in turn through the door that
led to my family's basement.

The room itself was a catalog of bad trends in seventies
decorating: Blond paneling surrounded a beige tile floor,
three striped sofas formed a semicircle in front of a color
television and a red shag rug, and my dad's autographed

photo of Bill Russell stood watch over a plastic ficus tree, hoping it, along with the rest of the room, might turn into something less ugly. This self-contained den occupied about a third of the basement. The rest was open space once devoted to a Ping-Pong table, but for the last few years playing host to Richie's drum kit and my amp.

The first bass player hopefuls were all kids we knew and any one of them would have been a fine replacement for Dave. We probably would have settled on Petey Havermayer—a short, sturdy kid with a deviated septum— if Cheyenne Belle hadn't walked in.

Cheyenne Belle.

She couldn't have stood more than five feet tall, and she couldn't have weighed more than ninety pounds soaking wet. The bass she held, a Rickenbacker, was large against her body, like a prop for a comedian parodying a race of tiny rock musicians. Her hair, the color of coal, was cut short in the back and left long in the front. Thick bangs hung down to her nose, obscuring one of her eyes, eyes so large that they looked like something out of a Disney movie. Cheyenne's features, other than those eyes, were like her physique—small, delicate, and fragile, waiting for a stiff wind to blow them away. She wore a boy's size, blue, button-down shirt, which hung loosely over tan short-shorts so close in color to the tone of her skin that at first glance she looked naked below the waist. Her outfit was completed by a pair of dusty red cowboy boots on the bottom, and a scaly red cowboy hat on top.

Johnny, Richie, and I were struck dumb. We were unable to talk, unable to move, unable to blink. A tiny smile crept on Cheyenne's tiny face and she said, "Where can I plug in?"

Johnny regained enough of his wits to point to the patch cord, one end lying on the floor at her feet, the other tethered to the second input on my amp. She looked at me as she plugged in, pausing a beat as we made eye contact. I don't know if she was examining my scars or just silently saying hello. Whatever it was, I wilted under her gaze and looked away.

Richie broke the silence. "Um, like, how old are you?"

"Old enough," she said in a way that closed the subject then and for all time. It turned out Cheyenne was our age, she was just cursed—or to my way of thinking, blessed— by those pixyish features. She attended Our Lady of the Perpetual I-Still-Can't-Remember-the-Name Catholic High School. How she heard about our audition, I never knew.

But the thing about Cheyenne that surprised us the most? She could play that bass like Jaco Pastorius. She responded to each new musical challenge we threw at her, playing the line we asked, and then improvising and improving it. For fifteen minutes we tried to trip her up, until it became a sort of game, finally coming to an end when one of the kids out in the yard opened the door and yelled downstairs, wanting to know if the auditions were over. They were.

We thanked Cheyenne and asked her to wait outside.

Johnny, our de facto leader, spoke first.

"Okay, she's in. But listen to me—none of us, not me, not you, not you," pointing at Richie and me in turn, "as long as we're in this band, can ever date this girl, kiss this girl, or sleep with this girl. She is off-limits. Agreed?"

Richie and I nodded.

Johnny would be the first to break this rule. I would be the last.

CHEYENNE

(written by Gary St. Clair and Tim O'Brien, and performed by Barry Williams, sometimes credited as The Brady Bunch)

From the moment Cheyenne joined the Scar Boys, things changed. Our rehearsals, our gigs, our music became infused with a new kind of energy. Maybe it was the sexual tension of having a girl in what had been an all-boys band, maybe it was hit-you-in-the-face rock and roll, or maybe it was something else. Whatever it was, it worked.

We thought we had gotten good with Dave in the band, and at some level, we had. We really had. But when Chey came along, it was like a whole new world opened up to us musically. She was the missing piece of our chemical equation. Everything seemed to go right when she was around. I broke fewer guitar strings, Richie broke fewer sticks, and Johnny hit notes beyond his range. We all settled into a groove and a confidence that worked like an amplifier. Not only did we get better, we got ten times better.

This new energy had a profound effect on me. For the first time since Johnny and I started the band, I took my hat, sunglasses, and denim jacket off, and I turned around to face the world. Yeah, sure, it was only rehearsal, with no one but the four of us there, but for me, it was a huge step. Or rather, it would've been a huge step if not for Johnny.

"Harry, what are you doing?"

The question was like a blow to my solar plexus. I practically doubled over in pain when Johnny asked it. Richie and Cheyenne stopped what they were doing to watch the exchange.

"What?" I answered. It wasn't really a question. It was more of an annoyed bark.

"Your disguise. You're taking it off?"

It didn't dawn on me at the time, but *disguise* was a carefully chosen word. It had the same effect on me that Darth Vader's "I find your lack of faith disturbing" had on *Star Wars* Expendable Guy Number Two. (In case, FAP, you're not well acquainted with the *Star Wars* canon—and shame on you if you're not!—Darth Vader uses his mind to choke Expendable Guy Number Two while uttering that phrase. It's awesome.)

"I dunno," I mumbled to my feet.

"Huh." That's all he had to say. *Huh*. Embedded in that word was everything between us. It said that I didn't get to make a decision like that on my own. That there were to be no big changes without the Johnny McKenna seal of approval. You have to understand that while Johnny didn't actually tell me what to do or not to do, everyone in the room knew exactly what his *Huh* meant.

I started to put the sunglasses and hat back on when Cheyenne cut in. She was looking straight at Johnny, but she spoke to me.

"Harry, you should leave them off. You have a beautiful face."

Johnny just shrugged and turned away. When he did, Chey turned to me. I was a deer caught in the headlights. I was a mounted, stuffed, decapitated deer caught in the god damn headlights.

"You should do what makes you comfortable, Harry. Don't listen to him."

If Richie or I had tried to defy Johnny like that, the result would have been an hour-long lecture on whatever the topic of that day was, on why we were wrong, and why he was right. Things didn't work that way with Cheyenne. No one, and I mean no one—not even Johnny McKenna— tangled with that girl.

The oldest of seven sisters, Cheyenne grew up in a Catholic household that was part *Carrie*, and part *Caddyshack*. Her mother went to church several times a week, mostly to pray for the soul of her father. He wasn't dead, he just smelled that way. The man's system had absorbed enough alcohol over the years to synthesize formaldehyde. Chey's dad didn't seem to know or care. He would just sit in his favorite chair, watch television game shows, and drink cheap brandy.

The influence of the Church at home was felt in the preponderance of crucifixes, Virgin Mary statues, and house rules—no boys, no makeup, no boys, no short skirts, no boys, no jewelry, and oh, yeah, no boys. But with her mom's devotion to Christ being a full-time vocation, and her father's devotion to the Christian Brothers being a full-time vacation, Chey and her sisters discovered early on that house rules were meant to be broken. For all the bluster religious people have about God and family, the Belle girls were raising themselves. They may as well have been orphans.

About a year after I met Cheyenne, her sister—fifteen years old—delivered a stillborn baby in her bed at home because no one knew she was pregnant. Don't ask me how a teenage girl can hide a nearly full-term pregnancy. Chey said that her sister was overweight to begin with, and that she wore a steady diet of peasant blouses, but I still had trouble believing it. Which was another thing about Cheyenne. You never quite knew when she was telling the truth.

It's not that she was a liar, just that she liked to stretch the facts to make a better story. When she told me that she stole her first bass guitar from the local music store, I took her at her word. I found out later that the bass was a rental that Cheyenne returned only after the store started legal proceedings for late payments.

As she stood there staring at me—my sunglasses and hat still in my hands—the only thing I could think was *Did she just say I have a beautiful face?* (Maybe Chey took liberties with the truth sometimes, but I never questioned her sincerity.)

I was about to put my costume on the floor, but then I caught Johnny's eye.

As smitten as I was with Cheyenne, Johnny still trumped everyone else. If he thought it was a bad idea, it was a bad idea. I put the "disguise" back on.

Cheyenne offered me a smile tinged with melancholy, and nothing else in my life has ever made me feel like more of a failure. I wanted to kill Johnny. Looking back, this was probably the beginning of the end for the Scar Boys, but I didn't know that at the time.

I launched into our next song, with perhaps a bit more intensity on the downstroke of my pick hand. I let my wrist take out some aggression on the strings, punishing them for the long list of things that were wrong with the world.

THESE BOOTS ARE MADE FOR WALKIN'

(written by Lee Hazlewood, and performed by Nancy Sinatra)

With the band graduating to new levels of musical prowess and interpersonal chemical connection, it didn't take long before we were ready to play out.

Johnny and Cheyenne took our new demo tape down to CBGB's and tried to convince Carol, the booking agent, to give us another chance. She did.

Having been through the pre-gig routine at CB's once already, we knew exactly what we were doing and what to expect. What we didn't expect, what I didn't expect, was the feeling I got from being onstage, on a real stage.

Playing in front of people was like a drug. The walls dropped away and I found myself surrounded by open air, floating above everything. The energy of the audience—even the tiny audience at that first gig—wrapped the entire band in a protective bubble. Only the music and the knowledge of each other existed. We were four individuals merged into one seamless being, each inside the other's head, each inside the other's soul. Music, I discovered that night, was a sanctuary, a safe place to hide, a place where scars didn't matter, where they didn't exist.

We didn't bring enough friends through the door to get a paying gig, but the soundman liked us, so they invited us back to play another showcase.

Besides the CBGB's gigs, we were playing Monday and Tuesday nights at the unsung clubs of Manhattan's Lower East Side—the Bitter End, R.T. Firefly, A7, and an aptly named dive called the Dive. These were the least desirable gigs in all of New York—the rooms were cramped, the bartenders were surly, and sound systems were seemingly hijacked from a White Castle drive-thru window—but they were gigs.

We got a small write-up in the *Village Voice*, and a DJ at WNYU, the only college station playing alternative music in all of New York City, had taken a shine to us, comparing us on the air to the Jam.

The more we played, the better we got. We eventually graduated from showcases to paying gigs, from Mondays and Tuesdays to Thursdays and Fridays. By the time we played our first Saturday night at CBGB's, in February 1986 and a little more than a year after Chey had joined the band, we'd started to gain a small but legitimate following.

We were the first of four bands on the bill that night, so we had to start our set at the ridiculous hour of eight o'clock. But even that early the room was wall-to-wall people, two hundred or more. It was by far the largest crowd we'd ever seen. When I strummed the opening notes of our first song, our friends and small but growing fan base gathered around the front of the stage like an eager congregation.

Richie and Cheyenne were in perfect sync. Their groove served as a polished steel backbone for the guitar and melody. The sounds screaming out of my big Peavey speakers were the exact blend of twang and balls I was always striving for but never quite seemed to nail. And Johnny moved and shook like he was possessed by the Holy Ghost.

In short, we kicked ass.

When we were called back for an encore, a palpable buzz made the walls of the nightclub shake. A coordinated throng of Lower Manhattan's rowdy and raucous punks— our thirty fans having swelled to two hundred disciples— hopped in unison and sang along as we lurched into our one and only cover tune, Nancy Sinatra's "These Boots Are Made for Walkin'."

Johnny practically made love to the mic with his low, sultry voice while the three of us scratched out a punk arrangement of the music. Cheyenne marched in lock-step to the snare drum, her red cowboy boots keeping time with the beat, the sole of each foot sliding in small rhythmic circles on the dusty planks of the CBGB's stage. Watching her had a physical effect on me—my palms and neck started to sweat, my sunglasses fogged up, and my heart, which was thumping along with the music, thumping along with Cheyenne, felt like it was going to explode.

Then the whole band stopped on a dime. Johnny hoisted the mic stand in the air and pointed it at the audience like he was holding a sword. Right on cue, each and every voice before us screamed out in unison:

ONE OF THESE DAYS THESE BOOTS ARE GONNA WALK ALL OVER YOU!

Johnny draped his arm around Cheyenne as her little hips swiveled and her fingers crawled down the neck of the bass, setting me up for one big, distorted power chord. Ever the showman, Johnny kissed Chey on the cheek the instant my pick hit the strings.

There were high fives all around as we leapt off the stage, retreating with our instruments to the dressing room for a drink of water before the frantic breakdown of equipment. We had to make room for the next band, a band with the dumbest name I'd ever heard: the Woofing Cookies.

The Cookies were from Georgia, touring the Eastern US on the strength of a 45-RPM single called "Girl from Japan." As I was coiling my patch cord and putting my guitar back in its case, the Cookies' drummer said with a pronounced drawl, "Hey ma-an, great set. Y'all oughtta come tuh Geoorgia."

It's funny how, to Yankee ears, a Southern accent on a woman sounds both charming and mysterious, a suggestion that a wild, untamed Scarlett O'Hara lurks beneath a praline-sweet exterior. A man with the same accent is a different story. He sounds slow, maybe a bit dim-witted. But if this drummer was talking with a regional dialect, I didn't notice. For all I knew or cared he was speaking with a British boarding school accent.

The road. Of course! We should go on the road!

TRAVELIN' BAND

(written by John Fogerty, and performed by Creedence Clearwater Revival)

I floated the idea of a tour on the ride back from the city.

"I was talking to that drummer from the Woofing Cookies," I began, as I drove north up the FDR Drive.

"Nice name," Johnny snorted.

"Yeah, but they totally rocked." Cheyenne had been mesmerized with their lead singer. It made me jealous as hell, and now I had the feeling it had been making Johnny jealous, too.

"Whatever," he said.

"Anyway, I was talking to him," I started again, "and he invited us to come play in Georgia, and it got me thinking, we should do a tour."

I don't know what I expected, but I didn't expect total silence.

. . .

. . .

. . .

. . .

. . .

. . .

And then . . .

"Fucking A!"

Richie bellowed so loud that I almost ran my parents' car off the road. Cheyenne, who was in the backseat next to Johnny, laughed and tousled Richie's hair. I added a few whoops and hollers of my own for good measure.

The three of us noticed all at once that something was wrong—Johnny wasn't laughing or whooping or hollering. He wasn't even smiling. He was silent and still, a department store mannequin in a bad mood. Our little celebration fizzled like a sparkler in the rain.

"What?" Richie asked. He was in the passenger seat and turned around to stare Johnny down.

"Well, I didn't tell you guys," he began, "but I've been offered a track-and-field scholarship to Syracuse and I accepted it. They're paying half my tuition."

This was the first time we'd heard anything about Johnny's college career. I knew he loved to run, but I thought he loved music more. This was tangible evidence that the Scar Boys might not last forever. It got very quiet very fast.

"I mean, you guys applied to colleges, too," Johnny said to Cheyenne and me. Neither one of us answered, because neither one of us had applied anywhere. I was done with school. I mean yeah, things had gotten better since I'd met Johnny and since we started the band, but to do it again, at a new school, with all new people? No thanks.

"C'mon," Johnny continued, "did you really think we were going to do this for the rest of our lives?"

And then it hit me: *Johnny was a tourist.* I'd been putting him on a rock-and-roll pedestal—he was the driving force behind the Scar Boys, the band was his idea, and he made most of the decisions. We were, or at least I believed we were, nothing without him. He was our David Byrne, our Iggy Pop, our Brian Eno. But all along he'd been posing as a rock star, playing dress up. As far as Johnny was concerned, we were just four kids from the suburbs who didn't have the right to think they could be anything more.

"Yeah," I mumbled, "that's exactly what I thought."

"C'mon Harry, get real. Do you have any idea what a long shot this would be?" He waved a dismissive hand at the three of us. "Grow up." Johnny could be such a jerk when he was trying to win an argument. I remember once, at a rehearsal, Johnny and I disagreed on a chord change in the bridge of a song we were working on. It started friendly enough, but after a few minutes, in one of the rare moments where I didn't immediately back down, Johnny got fed up and started saying "Blah blah blah blah" at the top of his lungs anytime I tried to talk. I would say "But I think—" and Johnny would say "Blah blah blah blah." I guess he thought he was being funny, but I mean really, who does that? It was enough to shut me up and we played the song Johnny's way.

So it wasn't a surprise that on the ride back from the CBGB's gig, I did what I always did when he went on the offensive—I crawled back into my shell.

"Even so," Cheyenne chimed in, "I kind of thought we were going to give this a try for a while." As was so often the case, Cheyenne was able to disarm Johnny with a simple, off-handed comment. Johnny didn't have a ready answer. When he finally opened his mouth to speak, Chey beat him to the punch. "Can't you defer?" She reached her hand out and very gently held his wrist. "This thing feels like it has momentum," she added. "What if this is, like, our one chance?"

Johnny was looking at Chey, trying to find something to say, when I saw a trace of pity in his eyes. He felt sorry for us. Johnny wasn't just a tourist, he was a Potsie. He had everything—popularity, good grades, parents that fawned over him—he didn't need this.

It was different for Richie, Cheyenne, and me. The band was a lifeboat, a way out. A way out of what? I'm not sure I know. But the three of us needed the Scar Boys like a methadone addict needs his junk, and I know something about that.

"What about Richie?" Johnny finally blurted out,

turning away from Chey and staring straight at me. Know-ing I was the weakest link, he focused his attention where he thought he could do the most damage. It was a trick my dad used all the time. Johnny was groping for any angle, any way to turn the discussion in his favor. "He still has a year of high school left."

"The school ain't goin' nowhere, John," Richie answered. "It'll be there when I get back. Besides, I'm not in school over the summer."

Johnny sat back. "The summer." He said it out loud. This was new information. He thought about it for another minute before saying it again, "The summer."

We were silent for a long time. The only sounds were "Radio Clash" coming from the car speakers and the occa-sional whoosh of passing traffic.

"Hey," Johnny said, sitting forward all of a sudden. It startled me. "I have an idea, let's do a tour in the summer."

Silence. No whoops, no hollers.

"Whaddya guys say?"

Yeah, the twit actually said all this without a trace of humor or irony. I'd come up with the idea of a tour, and Richie had come up with the idea of doing it in the sum-mer, but Johnny just pretended like this had been his show all along. The sick part is that we let him do it. The three of us just mumbled our agreement.

"Then it's settled. We'll do a tour and be back by the

middle of August so I can go to school." He clapped his hands together and smiled.

I hadn't been ready to admit it before that night, but Johnny had been falling steadily in my eyes for a while. Our relationship was breaking down ever so slowly. This, however, was a whole new low. In one short car ride, it felt like Johnny had gone from pedestal to poser. Don't get me wrong. He was still Johnny the leader, I was still Harry the follower, and he was still my best friend. But something had changed.

"But Harry," you might be asking yourself, "if Johnny was such a jerk, why did you keep hanging around him?"

Well, no offense, but if that's what you're wondering then maybe you haven't been paying close enough attention. Before I met Johnny, I didn't really know why I was alive. I don't mean to sound melodramatic or to suggest that I was suicidal—I wasn't—but do the math.

Friends? None.

Looks? None.

Athletic ability? None

Academic success? None.

Prospects? None.

Not to overstate it or anything, but in a lot of ways Johnny saved me. He was Vinnie Barbarino and I was Horshack. It was going to take something a lot bigger than this to finally blow us apart. But there I go getting ahead of myself again.

To me, Richie, and Cheyenne, the tour would be the start of an adventure. We would be Frodo, Sam, Merry, and Pippin heading out of the Shire. It wouldn't be the same for Johnny. He'd have one last party with the band and then head off to school. For him, the ride would end once and for all in August. I tried to convince myself otherwise, or at the very least I let myself believe that the tour would change Johnny's mind and make him see that this, the Scar Boys, was what we were all meant to do for the rest of our lives.

And in a way, that's exactly what happened.

WE WANT THE AIRWAVES

(written by Joey Ramone, and performed by the Ramones)

We had only a few months to pull a tour together, and our first order of business was to cut a record.

Since before Cheyenne joined the Scar Boys, we'd been hanging around the Mad Platter, a small, eight-track recording studio in Yonkers run by twin brothers, Dan and Don McAllister. Dan was Grizzly Adams—broad shoulders, thick red beard, a Zen-like confidence, and to us the very personification of wisdom. Don was the opposite— thin and twitchy, unable to locate his center.

The two had been the rhythm section for a modestly successful sixties garage band called the Pepper Mint, and had used the money they'd earned to found the Platter. With a hardwired soft spot for nurturing local bands, the twins let us barter for studio time. We painted ceilings, put up drywall, even helped finish the wood floors in the hallway. It was as much an education in carpentry and home repair as it was in sound engineering.

Over the years we'd recorded five songs at the Mad Platter, but the music was unproduced and amateurish— on tape we *sounded* like a bunch of kids from the 'burbs. We needed something better to press onto the vinyl that was to become the calling card for our tour.

When we approached the twins about recording a single, Dan (Grizzly Adams) apologized that there could be no barter this time. Bills at the Platter were mounting, and we were going to have to pay the rack rate of thirty dollars an hour. To do it right, he said, to lay down basic tracks, to do overdubs, to mix, remix, and remix again, to make it *great*, we would need as much time as ten hours per song. "Add in the cost of the tape, the artwork, and getting the singles pressed and shipped," Dan told us, "and you're looking at fifteen hundred dollars or more, soup to nuts."

We'd earned close to three thousand dollars playing gigs, most of which had been earmarked for transportation. But we had little choice. There was no sense in trying to book a tour without a record. We'd just have to find a less expensive ride.

The studio sessions at the Platter were everything we'd hoped they'd be. We recorded two songs: an anthem of sorts we'd been using to close our live set called "Assholes Like Us," and a pop tune called "The Girl Next Door."

I know, it's been said before
In every movie and Broadway musical score
But I'd give my right hand and my parents' car
And my left leg and my guitar
For just one night
With the girl next door

'Cause she's older than me and she's smarter than me
She's taller than me and that's how it should be
Just one night, with the girl next door

It was a song I had written about Leslie Murphy whose family lived two doors down from mine. She was four years older and babysat for me when I was a little kid. I had a monster crush on her that continued until she left for college. Strike that. The crush continues to this day.

Watching Johnny belt out the vocal from the iso booth, listening to the small flaws in his voice—the tiny bit of nasal inflection, the occasional drift off pitch—lay over the already recorded guitar, bass, and drum tracks like paint on wood, I knew, *I knew* without any trace of doubt that we were an unstoppable force.

The highlight was Dan's invention of the "stereo bells." He set up microphones on each end of the studio and had Richie run between them shaking a tambourine. The effect, other than to make Richie gasp for air and make us laugh ourselves stupid, was to hear the tambourine, when listening through headphones, moving from one side of your brain to the other. It was the crowning achievement on a record that was defined by whimsy.

The day the singles arrived—ten cartons of a hundred records each—was, and still is, one of the greatest days of my life. To hold in my hands the tangible fruit of five years' labor was an indescribable feeling. I imagined that this was what it must feel like to get laid. I can still remember the intoxicating smell of the ink on the jacket cover, a black and white photo of the band onstage.

We spent the better part of a week in my parents' basement stuffing envelopes and mailing the record with the *Village Voice* press clip to night clubs and college radio stations all across the country. Richie and Cheyenne spent the following week making phone calls. We had no idea how much an actual record would legitimize the Scar Boys, because in less than ten days, with what felt like a Herculean effort but in retrospect was really pretty easy, we had a tour. Twenty-three gigs through nineteen states in forty days.

Everything was falling into place. The only thing left to do was bag ourselves a set of wheels.

RIP OFF

(written by Marc Bolan, and performed by T. Rex)

Richie's dad—Alec, Mr. McGill, Mr. Mac—was a retired mechanic. He was a gruff man with thick hair shining an unnatural black from Grecian Formula, and skin turned to leather from years spent absorbing car exhaust. Mr. Mac barely came up to Richie's shoulder, but his hands were rough, scorched, and enormous. They were a source of wonder to me, large like a basketball player's, but nimble like a pianist's. He was the only one of my friends' parents who didn't seem uncomfortable with my deformities. He treated me like he treated any other kid, and I loved him for it.

"You're not gonna get much with thirteen hundred," he told us. Mr. Mac was on his hands and knees, his head under the sink, the sound of a wrench twisting, scraping, banging metal. I can't remember a single time at Richie's house when Mr. Mac wasn't busy working on something.

"Yes, sir, we know," Richie said. "Except, we already bought the van. It's out front. We're hoping you'll take a look."

The banging stopped and I could see Richie tense up. His relationship with his dad—a blend of respect, fear, and adoration—was so unlike the relationship I had with my own father, that it was kind of inspiring.

Richie's mom died when Richie was still in grade school. Stage four ovarian cancer. They say it doesn't strike women who've given birth, but someone forgot to tell Richie's mom's ovaries. Mrs. Mac—none of us had ever met her, but we all thought of her as Mrs. Mac anyway—woke up one morning with a pain in her back and a bloated feeling in her belly. Thinking she'd eaten something bad, or maybe tweaked a muscle, she did her best to muddle through the discomfort—going to work at the post office, picking Richie up after school, keeping the house clean, and resting when she could find the time. The hectic schedule of a suburban mom managed to hide, in very plain sight, her growing sense of fatigue. Richie's dad used his magical hands to massage her back, but that only seemed to make it worse, whatever *it* was.

Then one morning, Mrs. Mac woke up to find that the pain in her back had subsided, that it had faded to an echo of pain, there but not there. She figured she was on the mend. Three days later Mr. Mac came home to find his wife in bed with chills, aches, and fever, barely able to acknowledge his presence. Four weeks later, she was dead.

The pain in her back, Richie and his dad would later learn, was from a cantaloupe-sized, cancerous tumor pressing against her kidney. If Mrs. Mac had tended to it before it burst, the doctor explained, she might have had a chance. Once that softball of poisoned pus ruptured, and the cancer infected her kidneys, liver, and pancreas, it was game over. They tried surgery, but it was too late. Richie's mom died on the operating room table. There can never be a silver lining when something like that happens, but Mrs. Mac's absence did forge a bond between Richie and his dad that was unique among my friends, and I guess that counts for something.

"You did what?" Mr. Mac's head was still under the sink, and it was getting weird having a conversation with his butt.

"We bought a van. A Ford, sir. It's in the driveway."

"You bought it? A Ford?" Mr. Mac finally backed away from his work. "What the hell'dya do that for?"

"It was a great deal, Mr. Mac," Johnny chimed in. "Only 40,000 miles and the engine sounds real good." Mr. Mac looked at Johnny, then at the rest of us.

"Where's the girl?" We knew he meant Cheyenne.

"Not here, sir."

"Cars and shit are for boys," Cheyenne had said when we invited her along. "I'm going to treat myself to something 'girly' today." None of us knew what that meant, so when we caught up with her later we were surprised to find her crying and hiding her hands behind her back. Johnny coaxed her arms free and we found ourselves staring at two-and-a-half-inch long, pink-polished, buffed nails protruding from each finger—faux extensions of the real thing. "I can't even make a fist," Cheyenne sobbed. It took Richie and an acetylene torch forty-five minutes to remove them. How he didn't burn her hands to a crisp, I'll never know.

Mr. Mac sized us up and shook his head. "All right, let's go have a look."

In the McGills' driveway was a 1976 Ford Econoline van. It was powder blue, with two or three rust spots along the running boards. Inside were bucket seats finished in black vinyl, with a hard bench in the back that was flanked on each side by smallish windows. The spacious cargo area in the rear was more than enough room for the drums, guitars, amplifiers, and luggage we were going to bring on tour.

We'd found the van through an ad in the *Pennysaver*. "Cargo van. Runs good. $1300." Simple, direct, and the right price. Johnny called the number, and before we knew it we were forking over what was left of the band fund to an older black woman in a fine blue dress. She told us her husband had "used the van for his flooring business, God rest his soul," and that "he never drove it, as the good Lord is my witness, more than thirty-five miles per hour." For some reason, we believed her.

I bit my cuticles—a nasty habit I'd picked up from a need to keep my fingernails short for the guitar—while Mr. Mac rooted around under the hood of the Econoline.

"Start it up," he called to Richie, who did as he was told. Listening to the van's engine at Richie's house, under the scrutiny of his father's expertise, it didn't sound quite as good as when we'd driven it home. It sounded . . . congested. "All right, kill it." Mr. Mac emerged a minute later, wiping those enormous mitts on a filthy rag.

"Well, it's got 140,000, not 40,000 miles. And the catalytic's gone."

"Shit," Richie said, and then looked quickly at his father. "Sorry, sir."

"What does that mean, 'catalytic's gone'?" Johnny asked.

"It means we won't pass inspection," Richie answered.

"How much to get it fixed?"

"More than we have." The color drained from Richie's face and the room grew graveyard still.

Mr. Mac's frown softened and he rubbed his chin. He seemed to be staring at a blank spot in the sky. "I shouldn't do this," he said, "but there is another way."

CARS

(written and performed by Gary Numan)

Half an hour later we were leaving the quiet residential streets of northeast Yonkers behind, crossing the border into the Bronx. Mr. Mac had called an acquaintance who owned a garage on Jerome Avenue. "Gary the Grease Monkey" promised to give us an inspection sticker without actually inspecting the van. Fifty dollars was the price. Mr. Mac pressed three twenties into Richie's hand and sent us on our way.

The heart of the Bronx was a twenty-minute car ride from Yonkers, but it may as well have been on another continent. Like most people from the suburbs, my experience with the Bronx was limited to class trips to the zoo or botanical gardens. We saw the Bronx the way a Madison Avenue advertising executive saw the Midwest; you flew over without ever touching down.

The drive to Jerome Avenue was otherworldly. We were floating down Marlow's river, making our way deeper and deeper into an alien landscape, searching for an ever-elusive Mr. Kurtz. (That may be overdramatic, but we'd just read *Heart of Darkness* in English class, and hey, I want this thing to sound smart, don't I? It is a college essay after all.)

So yeah, I was afraid of the Bronx. Maybe it's why I'm a Mets fan. Where I lived—in safe, secure suburbia—retail stores didn't have steel shutters after dark, graffiti was the exception not the rule, and let's call it like it is, my corner of Westchester County was pretty white. I don't mean "pretty" white as in "nice-looking" white. I mean "pretty" white as in "where are all the people of color?" white. The Bronx was new to me, and like I had learned from Dr. Kenny, we fear what we don't know.

Of course, as harsh as life in the Bronx was supposed to be, the suburbs, I had learned firsthand, were no less cruel. I doubted that kids in the city were tied to trees during lightning storms. Chain-link fences maybe, but not trees.

Gary's garage was a dirty place, and I could see why he went by the name "Grease Monkey." An Irishman with a very light brogue (his last name was Gilligan), Gary was bathed in filth. From the point on his scalp where his hairline met his wrinkled forehead, to the tips of his stubby fingers, Gary was covered in a gelatinous layer of motor oil, brake fluid, steering fluid, grease, and exhaust, all of which had congealed into a kind of paste. When I asked Richie about it, he told me his dad came home from work looking like that every day, and only after a long shower with scalding water and Lava soap did he approach something you might consider clean.

We pulled the van into the garage and waited, watching as Gary dressed down one of his crew. The mechanic, a twenty-something black man who projected hostility, stood in silence as Gary called him every name in the book. We had no idea what the guy had done, but unless he'd run over Gary's dog, it couldn't have been bad enough to warrant the verbal beating he was taking.

When Gary was finished, he came over to us and said, "Gotta keep these boys in line, if you know what I mean," and winked. We didn't know what he meant, but we could guess. He'd said it loud enough for everyone in the garage to hear. No one reacted or looked at Gary or looked at us, but you could see the muscles on their necks and arms pull tight. I remembered something about Simon Legree from eleventh grade English class, and something else about Malcolm X from social studies. We paid our fifty dollars, got our sticker, and got out of there as quick as we could, making our way back to the safety of the suburbs.

By the time we got home, we were buzzing. From our sheltered point of view, our little adventure certified us as cool. The big, bad Scar Boys had braved and beaten the Bronx, and we had flouted the law in getting an illegal inspection sticker. We were invincible.

Uh huh.

Truth is, if we'd had a shred of sense, we'd have known we were getting in way over our heads. But you can't buy shreds of sense, and even if you could, we were pretty much out of money.

FEMME FATALE

(written by Lou Reed, and performed by the Velvet Underground)

The tour was all I could think about those last few months of my senior year in high school. While other kids were busy buying furniture for their dorm rooms and planning midnight keg parties at Jones Beach, I was dreaming of screeching guitars and sold-out shows.

Johnny was squarely in the former camp. On our nightly run, a ritual we had carried forward from the eighth grade, he talked more and more about Syracuse and less and less about the Scar Boys. It was depressing, but I kept my mouth shut.

Of course, that didn't stop Johnny from making sure that everyone in the twelfth grade—and most of the kids in the ninth, tenth, and eleventh grades—knew about our tour. He was using the tour to make himself cool, to satisfy his own massive ego, and it pissed me off.

On the other hand . . .

"Hi Harry. I heard your band is going on the road. That is so cool!"

Before that moment, and in the ten years since the lightning strike, Mary Beth Tice had said exactly six words to me. On three separate occasions she said, "Hi," and one other time she said, "Excuse me, please." That she had now chosen to more than double the word count of our entire life's conversation, in one fell swoop, was more than unexpected. It was mind-numbingly, disarmingly scary.

Mary Beth Tice was the "It Girl" at Theodore Roosevelt High School. She stood five feet six inches tall, had a trim body, and very symmetric features. She also had the greenest eyes I'd ever seen. They were like a satellite photo of the Amazon rain forest that we'd seen in Earth sciences class, full of mystery and life.

Most days she dressed down, wearing jeans and a T-shirt with her strawberry blond hair pulled back in a ponytail, and even then she was devastatingly beautiful. On the rare days that Mary Beth wore a skirt or a sundress, with her hair spilling over her shoulders, she would enter rooms in slow motion with a kick-ass soundtrack to accompany her every move. At least that's how I remember it.

To most of the male troglodytes in my year, "It Girl" simply meant they wanted to do "it" to Mary Beth. And while I don't think she was *that* kind of It Girl—in addition to her spectacular outer shell, she was smart (straight-A student), outgoing (class vice president), and funny (her imitation of our biology teacher had everyone in stitches, including the teacher)—she did know how to use her considerable gifts to her advantage. There was always a parade of boys trailing after her, carrying her books, doing her homework, lighting her "I-can-be-a-bad-girl-too" cigarettes.

It goes without saying that I wasn't one of those boys. I'd never done "it" to anyone other than myself. Heck, I hadn't even kissed a girl. Mary Beth was so far out of my league that she wasn't even in my dreams. Of course, I was still an incomprehensible idiot any time she came near me.

The three times Mary Beth said "Hi" to me (twice in the fifth grade and once in the sixth), I'd been the first kid to arrive in class for the day, and Mary Beth had been the second. She walked into the otherwise empty room and greeted me. It was, I suppose, a part of her DNA to acknowledge other forms of life. I remember taking particular solace that she hadn't also said hello to the two ferns that adorned the window ledge of the fifth grade classroom. On all three occasions I was too freaked out to respond.

The day she said, "Excuse me, please" (seventh grade), I'd been unwittingly blocking Mary Beth's exit from English class. When she approached, I froze, staying glued to the spot like I'd been stunned with a *Star Trek* phaser. She shrugged her shoulders and squeezed through the space between me and the door. I regained my wits and finally moved out of the way, but only after she was already a good fifteen feet past me. I added a sheepish, "Sorry." The other girls that had clustered around Mary Beth, hoping that some of her "Itness" would rub off on them, laughed at me. To her credit, Mary Beth ignored my gaffe and just kept on walking.

So why after a decade of invisibility had I suddenly materialized in front of Mary Beth Tice, as if out of thin air? Simple. If you're in a touring rock band, especially if you're still in high school, you are per se cool.

Unless, of course, you're the king of uncool.

Mary Beth was leaning against the locker adjacent to mine when she broke our ten-year vow of silence. At first, I presumed she was talking to someone else. It was the natural thing to think. Just like a fish had no reason to believe that the man on the boat was talking to it, I had no reason to believe Mary Beth was talking to me. Men didn't talk to fishes, and Mary Beth Tices didn't talk to Harbinger Joneses. It's not that I hadn't heard her, it's that I hadn't heard her talking *to me.*

I closed my locker, spun the dial, and turned to walk to class. The *"Hi Harry. I heard your band is going on the road. That is so cool!"* was still hanging in the air. It was static to me, white noise in the background. But there was Mary Beth

Tice blocking my way. Remembering the last time this'd happened—the day she'd said, "Excuse me, please" and I'd frozen—I acted quickly. I smiled and stepped to the side.

Then three things happened:

Thing #1: Mary Beth didn't move forward. In fact, she looked at me like I had two heads. (It's important to note that she did not look at me like I had one really ugly head. I know that look, and as a connoisseur of human facial expressions, I can tell you that this look was different.)

Thing #2: I noticed that her normal gaggle of devotees was absent, and that this month's boyfriend—Louie, the starting center for the football team—was nowhere to be seen. (You may be wondering why it is that I knew who Mary Beth's boyfriend was. If you are, then you might not be grasping the concept of an *It Girl*.)

Thing #3: I finally heard what she'd said and realized she'd been talking to me.

"Oh!" I said, with a little too much volume. "You were talking to me."

"Unless you know someone else who plays in a band that's going on tour?" she said in a teasing, and if I think about it now, flirtatious voice.

"Just Johnny and Richie," I answered, regretting my stupidity before the words were fully out of my mouth.

To her credit, Mary Beth smiled. I was dumbfounded. Mary Beth Tice didn't talk to me, and she definitely didn't smile at me. Something was amiss in the universe, and I stood there sullen and silent, trying to figure it out. Eventually, Mary Beth gave up. She got bored of waiting for me to make conversation, shrugged her shoulders, and walked away.

"Thanks," I managed to mutter when she was out of earshot. That's when I felt an elbow in my back and my face was slammed into the locker. It was Billy the Behemoth.

"Don't talk to yourself, freak. People will think you're crazy." He kept walking, his friends laughing out loud and high-fiving one another.

I may have been in a band, even a touring band, but I still occupied the bottom rung of the social ladder. It would take a lot more than a handful of gigs at a few out-of-town nightclubs to change that.

So let's move on. No wait. Before we do, let's take a step back. It's important to the story. Trust me, you'll see.

FATHER AND SON

(written and performed by Cat Stevens)

When I was a kid—before there was ever a Johnny McKenna or a Cheyenne Belle or a Ford Econoline van—my mother, father, and I would spend one week each summer on a spit of sand just off the New Jersey coast called Long Beach Island. I would sit on that beach for hours, a hooded sweatshirt hiding my face from the other kids, and watch wave after wave build and break. The thundering sound of the surf, rather than upsetting me the way real thunder did and does, soothed me, made me believe I wasn't afraid of anything.

During these vacations—and always at my insistence—we'd pay a visit to the century-old Barnegat Lighthouse at the northern tip of the island. I was obsessed with that lighthouse. I knew everything about "Old Barney," from the date he was built to the date he was decommissioned. I'd look up at his red and white tower and admire his strength and solitude. I'd wish that I could be a lighthouse, too.

Leaden clouds blanketed the sky from horizon to horizon as we stepped out of the car on one particular afternoon in 1979. I was craning my neck to stare at the top when something wet and cold nudged the back of my leg, startling me to the point of almost falling over. I turned around to find a beagle-lab-something-or-other mutt looking up at me, tail wagging, eyes full of expectation. I bent down to pet him and he licked my hand. The little guy didn't have a collar. I scanned the parking lot but didn't see anyone who looked like they were missing a dog.

"Mom?" My mother turned and saw the two of us standing there, probably both looking lost. If I'd had a tail I suppose it would have been wagging, too.

"Oh, isn't he precious. Ben, come over here."

To understand what happens next, you have to know two things about my father:

First, he'd grown to resent me. From the moment my mom found my flaming body dangling from that dogwood tree, my dad had become the odd man out in our house. Everything in my mother's world revolved around me. She had no attention and no patience left for her husband. My dad dealt with it for a while, but eventually he got fed up. I would overhear my parents late at night, my father complaining that their life had come to a complete standstill, that they were starting to lose their friends, that it wasn't healthy for them or for me. My mother, sounding shocked, would only say "But Ben . . . Harry!" A few months later the bickering turned to arguing, their voices reaching a decibel level that even a pillow held smushed over my head couldn't keep out. After that they gave up all pretense and fought out in the open. If you're from a happy home, you just can't know how much this sort of thing sucks.

It didn't help that my father was out of work at the time. A local news station had videotaped my dad's latest political patron, a New York City councilman, coming out of a drag bar. He—the councilman, not my dad—was wearing a frilly green dress, matching shoes, and pearls. The photo beneath the *Daily News* headline, which read "Council Woe-Man," showed my dad's boss in the full getup, but without his wig. The story mushroomed into a citywide scandal, which, like all scandals, blew over as soon as the newspaper-reading mob moved onto the next big thing. But the damage was done. The councilman was forced to resign, and my dad was left to putter around the house and get in my mom's way.

There's an apocryphal story about my dad wanting to wash his boxer shorts in their new top-loading Maytag dishwasher, the first either of them had ever owned. "Ruth, if it cleans the glasses, it will clean the clothes." My mom gave him a choice: find a job, or else. He didn't know what "or else" was, and he didn't wait around to find out.

My dad took a job working as a legislative liaison in the governor's office in Albany, three hours away. We'd see him on weekends, at Christmas, during summer vacation, and most other times the legislature was out of session. He'd barrel into the house like a freight train, showing up with souvenirs from around the state: A refrigerator magnet from Skaneateles Lake, a "Relax at the Spa" button from Saratoga, a T-shirt with a picture of the *Maid of the Mist* in the foreground and a rainbow and Niagara Falls in the background.

The long-distance living arrangement seemed to solve the problem for my mother, but it never suited my dad, or maybe it never suited his idea of what his life should be like. My father imagined himself the king of his castle, a benevolent, enlightened man, presiding over life at his own Kennedy compound. Instead, he was an exile, granted visitation only when the government allowed, and he blamed it all on me. It was a feeling that had been gnawing at him and it needed an outlet.

The second thing to understand about my dad is that he really hates dogs.

My father was just about to go into the lighthouse when he heard my mother call. He walked over to where we were standing.

"I think he's lost," I said, motioning to the dog.

"Nonsense. He's with one of these families. Someone is up in the lighthouse and they just left him to wait."

"I don't know, Ben," my mother said, studying the dog.

My father muttered "For crying out loud" to himself, and, always desperate to prove his point, stomped off, systematically approaching the few other families in and around the lighthouse while my mother and I waited. Five minutes later he came back with his brow furrowed.

"One of the men inside saw a green station wagon pull up, let the dog out, and drive away. They think maybe he was abandoned here."

"Oh, how awful." My mother looked at my father with pursed lips, motioning at me with her eyes. "We can't just leave him here."

"What exactly are we supposed to do?" my father asked, his words clipped.

"Can we keep him?" I knew the answer before it was spoken.

"Absolutely not."

"We can at least bring him to a shelter, dear."

My father weighed his options, knowing that if he did nothing he'd spend the rest of his vacation with a sullen, angry wife and a disappointed son. He grudgingly agreed. "Okay, a shelter."

Dad got down on his hands and knees a few feet from the dog and whistled, trying, I supposed, to mimic something he'd seen in a movie or on TV. "C'mere boy, over here." The dog, who in my head I'd given the clever name of "Blacky," wasn't buying it. He inched back.

My father inched forward.

Blacky inched back.

My dad stood up and looked around, pretending to ignore the dog, thinking he could outsmart him. The dog never took his eyes off my father, so when Dad lunged forward to grab him, Blacky bolted.

In the instant the dog turned and ran, I heard a sickening scrape of bone on bone and I saw my father grab his back and fall to the ground. The pain must have been intense, because tears were streaming down his lobster-colored cheeks, and his breath was short and raspy. I held out my hand to help him up, but he batted it away.

"This is your fault, everything is your fault! Just get away from me you god damn freak!"

. . .

. . .

. . .

. . .

. . .

. . .

. . .

. . .

. . .

. . .

. . .

. . .

. . .

. . .

. . .

. . .

. . .

. . .

. . .

. . .

. . .

. . .

. . .

. . .

. . .

. . .

. . .

. . .

. . .

. . .

. . .

. . .

. . .

. . .

. . .

. . .

. . .

. . .

. . .

. . .

. . .

There was no wind, no sound of the ocean, no sunlight. Just the reverberating echo of the word "freak" as it ricocheted off the lighthouse and the rocks in the flat, gray stillness.

"Ben!" my mother barked and time started moving forward again.

My father mumbled something, I didn't know what, and took my hand, which was still extended in his direction. I didn't even think about my reaction. I pulled his arm as hard as I could, jerking his torso and head toward my foot, which was moving in the direction of his face at the speed of sound. When my Converse sneaker connected with his mouth, I felt something crack. Three bloodstained teeth flew through the air and landed on his chest. I dropped knee-first onto his solar plexus, knocking the wind out of him. His arm was still in my grasp when I landed, and I could feel his shoulder separate.

Strike that. I couldn't feel his shoulder separate or anything else, because, no matter how much I might've wanted to, that's not what I did.

Here's what really happened:

My father mumbled something, I didn't know what, and took my hand, which was still extended in his direction. I helped him up. He didn't look me in the eye, and he didn't say anything else. I was so used to dealing with crap like this at school that I knew how to control and bottle up my emotions. I just pretended like it'd never happened. I didn't even let myself cry.

I opened the car door for the old man, preparing to ease him into the backseat, when, without warning, the dog came bounding across the pavement and leapt in ahead of us, his tail wagging so fast it was just a black blur. My father hurled some insult at Blacky, and I did my best not to laugh.

After we dropped the dog at the local shelter, my dad spent the rest of the vacation lying prone on the floor of our bungalow. It was the beginning of a lifelong battle with back spasms, his vertebrae shifting without warning into configurations so painful as to require a cane for support.

He did apologize that night, looking up at me from the floor. A well-worn carpet surrounded him, making it look like he was floating in a beige-colored sea. He told me that sometimes, in the heat of a crisis, people say and do things they don't mean to say or do.

"Pain and stress can hijack a man's soul and twist it out of shape, like my back," he said, trying to smile.

I nodded, but it didn't matter, the damage was done. I didn't believe his excuse anyway. My sorry little life had already taught me that things said under duress are always more true than not. But there was at least one unintended consequence from that vacation. I had the moral high ground and a "Get Out of Jail Free" card with my father.

LYING

(written and performed by the Woofing Cookies)

It was a Friday afternoon. My dad was home from Albany for the weekend and we were sitting across the kitchen table from one another. I was leaving on tour in a matter of weeks, and I hadn't told my parents anything about it. In fact, regarding my future, I had told them a series of colossal lies.

Colossal Lie #1: I had applied to four colleges. They'd helped me fill out the applications, write my essays, and even took me to see all four schools. When everything was ready to be mailed, I drove my mom's car to the post office—"Mom, Dad, this will mean more to me if I'm the one to mail the applications"—and pitched all four packages in a Dumpster.

Colossal Lie #2: I was accepted at the University of Scranton, my first choice. Johnny had applied to Scranton as a safety school and got in. He was too much of a choir-boy to want to give me his acceptance letter and packet of admissions materials, but Cheyenne talked him into it. A little creative cutting, pasting, and photocopying, and I made it look like the package was addressed to me. I'd never seen Mom and Dad more proud.

Colossal Lie #3: I mailed the check my dad wrote to Scranton—for the first semester tuition, room, and board—to the same place I'd "mailed" the application, though I was smart enough to tear the check into little pieces before throwing it away.

It was against this fictional backdrop that I told my father I was going on the road.

"We'll be gone about a month."

"But that means you'll be late going to school," he said, a bit bewildered. I'd caught him off guard, which was my plan.

"It'll be fine. I'll be there for the first day of classes."

There must've been something in my voice, because my dad did a double take. His eyes narrowed, and his usually fidgety hands went very still. His Spidey sense was working.

"Harry, how long have you been planning this? You said you have a van, you made a record, and you booked more than twenty shows, that's not something you do overnight, is it."

"I don't know, I guess a couple of months."

"And why didn't you tell me sooner?"

"I was afraid you'd say no."

"But what if I say no now?"

I was silent because we both knew the answer. I was going with or without his blessing. But he was digging for something else here.

"You know, the check we sent to Scranton hasn't been cashed yet."

This is the scene in the movie where the prisoner has just escaped from the cellblock and is skulking along the interior perimeter of a giant brick wall when a massive floodlight stops him in his tracks. Busted.

"Huh," I said, trying to act cool, "that's weird."

"I should say so. Tell me, Harry, if I call the school and ask why, what do you think they'll tell me?"

Stick with the lie, I told myself, *ride it all the way to the end.* "Probably some clerical mistake," I said. "I'll call them for you and find out."

"Aha!" He pointed at me. My offer to call, or rather my effort to stop him from calling, was the clue he was looking for. "You never mailed the check, did you? You used that money for your band's little tour!" When he got angry his Boston accent became more pronounced. The "a" in band was flattened, and "tour" became "taw."

"No! Dad, I wouldn't steal from you! Besides," I said, thinking fast, "if I'd used the check, it would've been cashed, right?" This calmed him down a bit.

"Hmm. Yes, yes, I can see where that would be true." But he still wasn't convinced. "Then what happened to it?"

"Really, Dad, I don't know. I'll call the school and find out."

"No, Harry, I'll call the school." He went to his home office to get the phone number and make the call, leaving me in the kitchen to sit and think.

I figured I had three options:

Option #1: Run. Get out of the house and get on tour. Things would sort themselves out. Only problem was, all our gear was in my parents' basement. And I had nowhere to go and nowhere to hide for the three weeks until the tour started.

Option #2: Go find my dad right then and there and confess. Do it before he makes the call and maybe he'll go easy. Tell him everything and let the chips fall where they may.

Option #3: Wait it out. Let an opportunity present itself to me.

I chose door number three.

Five minutes later my father came back into the kitchen. I was still sitting at the table. I didn't look up.

"Isn't that strange," he said.

"Did they get the check?" I asked.

"Why you cheeky little bastard," he said. I kept my head down. "You lied about everything, didn't you?"

No answer from me. I kept my eyes glued to the Formica surface of that kitchen table.

"The school has never heard of you. Not even an application. You've been playing this charade for months. For the first time in my life I wish I was a violent man so I could beat the living daylights out of you." My dad was just getting wound up. When he stumbled into a morally righteous position, all bets were off. His paternal soul gave way to his political mind as he figured out how best to eviscerate me.

I sat there with my head down as my father spewed a rainstorm of abuse on me. I was so wrapped up in my own world, trying to figure a way out, that I only caught sporadic words and phrases from his rant.

"Ingrate."

"Thankless."

"We sacrificed everything for you."

"Toaster." I looked up at that one, not sure how a toaster figured into what he was saying, but he was so lost in the brilliance of his own argument that he hardly noticed I was still there. It went on and on and on and on.

Then I heard "failure," and "loser" in rapid succession. He was probably saying something like "I don't want you to be a failure," and "Don't end up as a loser," but I didn't hear the context and the words were like a trigger. I'd had enough. It was time to play my one and only card.

"You're right, Dad," I interrupted him with an edge. My tone caught his attention and I could see that he was shocked I was talking back. "I guess it's just what us *god damn freaks* do, isn't it." I met his eyes and held his gaze. *Let him stare at my mangled face*, I thought. *Let him see his son.*

My dad knew exactly what I was saying. He was the only person on the planet with a more vivid and more painful memory of that day at the lighthouse than me. He knew this was my golden ticket, that there was nothing he could say. And I knew this wouldn't work for me more than once. At least my deformities had taught me how to choose my battles.

He started to say something almost a full minute later, but then thought better of it. He flopped down into a chair. And just like that, it was over. I had won.

GONE DADDY GONE

*(written by Willie Dixon and Gordon Gano,
and performed by the Violent Femmes)*

A few days after school ended we were loading equipment into "Dino," the name with which we'd christened the Econoline. We made trip after trip from my parents' basement and through the garage to the open and waiting cargo doors of the van.

We carried our cymbals stands, guitars, and amps past the lawn mower, the beach chairs, and the old Schwinn; around the tin saucer used for sledding, the bucket and brush and Rain Dance for washing cars, and the fifty-foot coiled snake of green garden hose; and over a haphazard collection of rakes, shovels, and sawed-off two-by-fours. My father stood guard, trying, but failing, not to scowl each time one of us went by. He was dressed in khaki shorts, a brightly colored, striped polo shirt, and boat shoes. A "NY State National Guard" hat covered his thinning hair. The skin on his exposed legs was translucent white, his veins and arteries tracing obvious lines down the length of his shin. He leaned on a golf putter, using it as a cane to support his ailing back.

My mom was in the house crying. I knew this because when I went in to say good-bye, she lost it. She wrapped me in a bear hug and didn't want to let go.

"I know your father is upset," she told me, "and you shouldn't have lied to us. But Harry?"

"Yeah Mom?"

"I'm so incredibly proud of you."

That's when the waterworks started, from both of us. I hugged her again, and she shooed me away. I composed myself and went back outside.

Cheyenne was walking out with her bass, and that was it. We were packed and ready to go.

"We're all set, I guess," I said to my dad. "See you in a month." His stern gaze stopped us all in our tracks.

"Remember," he said very seriously and very suddenly, "think with the head on your shoulders." We must've seemed confused because he added, "Not you, Cheyenne." Then he shoved a small wad of bills into my hand, and disappeared into the house. I shrugged my shoulders and turned away.

It was probably the most personal and tender moment my father and I ever shared, and I clung to it the way a dying man clings to a priest's robes. The advice and the money were proof that his love was unconditional—twisted and weird proof, but proof just the same. And like the Grinch, my heart, at least the way it felt about my dad, grew a size or two that day.

Then my father was gone and the gears in my brain lurched back to the Scar Boys. We piled into Dino, certain we were ready for whatever the world was going to throw at us.

Richie was driving the first shift with me in the passenger seat. Johnny and Cheyenne were in the back, their knees, elbows, and shoulders touching. Chey was affectionate like that—a light touch on the bicep, a passing squeeze of a shoulder muscle, even the occasional peck on the cheek was par for the course. When I was the lucky recipient, which wasn't often, it was the highlight of my day. I would lie awake at night remembering her touch, no matter how insignificant, and dream about the next time it would happen. Strike that. I would dream bigger dreams, dreams of Chey and me together, of going to movies, going to dinner, holding hands, kissing. I knew it was a fantasy, but as long as she gave those small, physical cues, there was hope. And hope is a dangerous thing. But in the weeks leading up to the tour she'd stopped all signs of affection with everyone except for Johnny.

I pretended not to notice.

I turned the radio on as we drove down my parents' street into an uncertain future. One of the only AM music stations left on the dial was playing "Join Together" by the Who. I took it as an omen that big things were in store for the Scar Boys.

STREETS OF BALTIMORE

(written by Tompall Glaser and Harlan Howard, and performed by Gram Parsons)

"You were awesome, dude," Richie said to me. It was fourteen hours after we'd left Yonkers and we were sitting in an all-night diner in Baltimore, congratulating each other on what we thought was a great first gig on the tour. "I don't know how you got the feedback coming out of your amp to screech like that, but man, I could feel it in my sneakers."

I just smiled. It *was* a great gig. There weren't a whole lot of people there, but that didn't matter.

The four of us were sharing two plates of French fries in brown gravy; something we had never tried before, but that the waitress had assured us was a Maryland delicacy. It was good, but because we thought it was exotic and cool, we were convinced it was incredibly, unbelievably, maniacally good. That was the feeling we all had that night.

The gig had been in the back of a bar in the Pimlico

section of the city, close to the racetrack, and closer still to check-cashing, gold-buying, and liquor-selling storefronts, all of them covered with steel shutters at this hour.

We were one of three bands on the bill, and other than the manager of the first band and the girlfriend of the drummer in the second band, the only people in the bar seemed to be neighborhood regulars. They sat on their stools with their baseball caps pulled low; they gave off a vibe of being pissed off. Either the owner of the bar was lousy at promoting gigs, was trying live music for the very first time, or there was somewhere a whole lot better to be in Baltimore that night.

We were the first band to take the stage, and no one seemed to care. The neighborhood regulars sipped their drinks and didn't do much else. But as we played deeper into our set, we saw their attention shift from the TV sus-pended above the bar to us. Before long toes were tap-ping, heads were bopping, and faces were smiling. When we finished, we got a nice round of applause. There was no encore, but the mood in the room was unmistakably good.

"You know," Cheyenne offered as she scooped up a gelatinous glob of gravy, "a night like tonight is the reason I joined this band in the first place."

"Not me," Richie said, tongue firmly in cheek. "I'm in it for the chicks." Johnny and I laughed.

"All I've ever wanted," Chey continued, ignoring us, "is

to play music that would make people feel good. We did that tonight." We were all quiet for a moment.

It's funny. I'd never really thought of it that way before. I'd only ever thought about how playing music made me feel. But Chey was right. The real magic comes from the audience. Music, it turns out, is more about giving than receiving. Who knew?

"I've always wondered," Johnny asked Chey, "why did you want to play the bass?"

"I didn't." She didn't offer more. That's how Chey was. An enigma, wrapped in a riddle, covered by a blanket or whatever the hell that phrase is.

"Then why do you?" Johnny persisted.

"Because I can't play the trumpet." We all looked at her sideways, which is pretty much what Chey wanted, and she laughed. "I started playing the trumpet in the fifth grade. All the other girls chose the flute or clarinet, but I didn't want to be like the other girls. I wanted to be one of the boys, so I took up the trumpet." Again, Chey stopped, like we were supposed to know the rest of the story. Like we'd all read her biography.

"And?" Johnny asked.

"Braces."

"Braces?" Richie asked.

"My teeth were crooked. I got braces. I had to give up the trumpet."

"Okay," Johnny said, "but why the bass? Why not the piano, or guitar?"

"How the hell should I know?" Chey was annoyed that Johnny had finally gotten to the heart of the matter, had pierced her protective shell of misdirection and confusion, and he let it drop. This was classic Cheyenne. Anytime the conversation turned to her, she would run you in circles, and just when you thought you were getting somewhere, she would leave you scratching your head harder than when you started. It drove us all nuts, and made us all like her even more.

"How about you, Harry, what's in all of this for you?" Cheyenne asked, waving her hand at the four of us.

I didn't know what to say. I'd joined the band because Johnny had wanted to start a band. He was my first, and at the time, only friend and I would have joined the circus if he'd thought it was a good idea. But now that I was here, I couldn't imagine doing anything else. I'd stumbled onto my one true love, music, as an accident of circumstance.

"I don't know," I finally answered. "I guess I didn't have anything better to do."

Johnny snorted. "For me, it's always been about the music," he said with a little too much force. I didn't believe him. It sounded like the kind of thing Johnny would say so people would think he was smart, or wise, or sincere.

But I was in too good of a mood for Johnny being Johnny to spoil it.

When I look back now, sitting in that diner was the last really happy memory I had of that tour and everything that came after.

BREAKDOWN

(written by Tom Petty, and performed by Tom Petty and the Heartbreakers)

The swollen Virginia sun was beating down on the van, and the air conditioner—a truly fine piece of machinery designed by the brilliant engineers of the glorious Ford Motor Company—barely kept the inside temperature under eighty degrees. It was our third day on the road, and we were on our way to a radio interview at the University of Richmond. Richie was driving, with me in the passenger seat. Johnny and Cheyenne were in the back, she with her legs draped across his lap. I'd continued my self-delusion that each new sign of affection between the two of them was platonic and that we were really one big happy family. It was getting harder and harder to believe my own lie, but I was determined.

A brittle SNAP! came from under the van.

Richie grabbed hold of the wheel and muscled us over to the curb.

"Dammit! Cotter pin!" he exclaimed. He hit the hazard lights and leapt out the door. I looked back at Johnny who shrugged his shoulders. We all climbed out.

We were stopped on a narrow two-way street with no room for parking. Cars were able to move around us, but had to slow down enough that we were causing a traffic jam. Richie had the cargo doors open and was rooting around in his drum gear.

"What the hell's going on? What's a cotter pin?" Johnny demanded.

"The clutch," Richie answered, not looking up from what he was doing. I saw a bit of his father in him, tolerating the need for conversation, but focusing his attention on the work his hands must do. "When I stepped on the clutch to change gears, it went straight to the floor, lost all its tension. That noise you heard?"

"Yeah?"

"It was the cotter pin —a little piece that connects the clutch to the gears — breaking off."

"How can you possibly know that?" Johnny demanded.

"Dude," Richie answered, still rooting around in his gear, "when you have a mechanic for a dad, you just know."

"So what do we do?"

"We fix it." Richie turned around, holding a coat hanger in one hand and a pair of needle-nose pliers in the other. "Never be without one of these," he smiled, waving the hanger in our faces. He reminded me of Ford Prefect extolling the virtue of always carrying a towel, seconds before the Earth was destroyed. (I'm just going to assume, FAP, that you're cool enough to know about *The Hitchhiker's Guide to the Galaxy*.)

Without another word, Richie dropped to his knees and rolled under Dino, his legs swinging out into traffic as he reached into the engine. The three of us were left to wave cars around.

As is true every summer afternoon south of the Mason-Dixon, the stifling heat and humidity were nature's bit of foreshadowing. In those few minutes between the snapping of the cotter pin and Richie's disappearance beneath the van, roiling clouds crept in and blotted out the sun.

The first few raindrops coincided with the first flash of still far-off lightning. I silently counted—*one Mississippi, two Mississippi, three Mississippi, four Mississippi, five Mississippi, six Mississippi, seven Mississippi, eight Mississippi, Nine*—and then the unfurling of low, rumbling thunder. *Almost two miles away.*

I caught Cheyenne looking at me when she heard the thunder and I could see she was worried. Chey knew my history, and knew that I made a point of staying away from bad weather. When I met her gaze she reached for me. Her hand was tiny and soft, the fingertips, like mine, were calloused from playing the bass. But on Cheyenne even the calluses were smooth and gentle. Her hands were the antithesis of Mr. Mac's. His oversized first baseman's mitts were tools to make and unmake the world. Cheyenne's were slender silk gloves made to stroke, caress, and save it.

On some level I understood this was a maternal act. I was one of her family, one of her cubs, and she was protecting me without knowing why. But I was also an eighteen-year-old boy, a lonely eighteen-year-old boy with untested hormones, and even though I hadn't admitted it to myself, I'd been in love with this girl since the moment she walked into my parents' basement.

Maybe my pupils dilated, or my mouth twitched, or the muscles in my forearm tensed, because Chey gave my hand a gentle squeeze and let go. "It's okay if you want to wait in the van," she said.

"I'll be fine."

There were six "Mississippis" between the next bolt of lightning and the next boom of thunder, this one a little less rumble and a little more crackle. The sky, stained a dirty but glowing green, had given itself completely to the encroaching storm. The electricity in the air made the hairs on my arm stand on end and I felt myself losing what little control I had. The panic started to overwhelm me. But it wasn't panic about thunder and lightning, at least it didn't play out that way. That's the thing about panic attacks. They're never what they seem. Most of the time you don't know why you're freaking out. I suppose if you did, you wouldn't be having a panic attack.

I robotically waved cars by and started to wonder what the hell I was doing there, standing on the side of a road in Virginia, in the pouring rain, our piece of crap van giving in to its piece of crap nature, tortured by the unrequited love of a girl never more than five feet away but who may as well have been on Easter Island, waiting for a gig in a town where no one knew or cared who we were, chasing some idiotic dream I had no business chasing. I should've been home. I should've been getting ready to go to college. I should've had a job at Caldor's or McDonald's or the movie theater. I should've been going on dates. I should've been doing what all the other kids my age were doing.

A flash of lightning. *One Mississippi, two Mississippi, three*—the thunder starting with that staticky sizzle that said *I'm here Harry, and I'm coming for you*, setting up the cannon blast. BOOM! I flattened myself against the van and shut my eyes.

But I wasn't all those other kids. I was different. I was a freak. I couldn't work in Caldor's or McDonald's or the movie theater. I couldn't go on dates. I was never going to get the girl. Or the job, or the money, or anything else. College was just going to be high school all over again with me the misfit. The misfit, not fitting, standing apart, alone, outside. Outside. A searing white light penetrated my eyelids, eyelids that were shut so tight that light shouldn't have made it through the skin and muscle to my optic nerve, shouldn't have been able to travel the length of that nerve to the neurons in my brain, the brain that was screaming for me to get the fuck out of there.

One Missi—the explosion. A tree branch down the street shattering and falling to the ground. I didn't see it, I heard it. I could *hear* that it was a dogwood tree, I could *feel* it catching fire. The rain was pouring down my face. Not a cleansing rain, a damning rain.

Hands. Cheyenne's small delicate hands. More hands. Rougher, masculine. Pulling me, guiding me. My Converse high-tops soaked through, my socks soaked through, my skin soaked through, my bones wet. I allowed myself to be led, but didn't open my eyes until those hands were helping me through the side door of the van. I crawled onto the bench in the back and balled myself up like a fetus. Cheyenne and Johnny climbed in next to me.

"I'm all right," I managed to mutter. "Sorry." I listed Beatle albums, with songs, in chronological order, to calm myself down. I began with *Introducing the Beatles*: "I Saw Her Standing There," "Misery," "Anna," "Chains . . ."

Richie climbed in the front seat. He was drenched from head to toe, his face so smudged with grease and oil that he looked like something out of *Apocalypse Now*. He started the van, carefully depressed the clutch, and pulled the shift on the column into gear.

"Fucking A!" he screamed, as the gears engaged and we rolled on down the road.

WHAT A FOOL BELIEVES

(written by Michael McDonald and Kenny Loggins, and performed by the Doobie Brothers)

No one stopped us as we sprinted through the student union on the University of Richmond campus, racing to get to WDCE in time for our interview. I can only imagine what we looked like, with our drenched clothing, Richie's blackened cheeks, and my own face, sideshow that it was. I'm surprised no one called the cops.

When we found the station, the actual studio was too small for the whole band, so Johnny and Cheyenne did the interview while Richie and I waited outside. This arrangement was never discussed. It just happened. This was Johnny after all. He was the front man. He was the voice. He was the leader. But this was also Johnny the tourist, the Potsie, Mr. Future College Boy, and it pissed me off.

It's not like I wanted to do the interview. Hell no.

I'd sooner have walked naked down a busy street. I just wished we'd talked about it first.

The three of them had tried to console me on the ride over to the campus, filling the van with one platitude after another. "It's only natural, Harry, someone who's been through what you've been through can't help but have that reaction." (Johnny) "We're a family, Harry. We all love you. You have nothing to be embarrassed about with us." (Cheyenne) "Don't sweat it, dude. Lightning never strikes the same place twice." (Richie)

Richie and I sat in the reception area, listening to the broadcast through speakers suspended from the ceiling. I traced a circle on my palm, feeling the outline of where Cheyenne's hand had touched mine during the storm. That only made things worse.

DJ: *So why "The Scar Boys"?*

Johnny: *Our guitarist picked the name. He was struck by lightning as a kid, and it left him with a few scars.*

DJ: *Struck by lightning, really?*

Johnny: *It's the truth.*

DJ: *Don't you think that brings you bad luck?*

Johnny: *Just the opposite. Like Richie, our drummer, always says, no one ever gets struck by lightning twice.*

Cheyenne: *Though I suppose he could get electrocuted onstage.*

I listened as the three of them—Johnny, Cheyenne,

and the DJ—clucked insincere, staged chuckles, laughter without feeling, laugh-track laughter. And I convinced myself right then and there that I was and had always been nothing more than the Scar Boys' gimmick. I was a prop.

The radio interview managed to get a handful of people out to the club that night, which was a handful more than the first gig on the tour. They were with us by the third song, on their feet and dancing. I let the music revive me and felt my emotional funk fade. The alder wood of my guitar vibrated against my stomach. It was the same sensation as feeling a cat purr and it calmed me down. I closed my eyes and lost myself in the groove.

Later, packed, loaded, and ready to go, we decided we needed a night in a hotel. It'd been three nights sleeping in the van, and we were starting to get rank. Richie guided Dino back to the highway and then off the very first exit where we found a sea of budget motor inns. With the money my dad had given me burning a hole in my pocket, we booked two rooms. Johnny, Richie, and I retreated to one, Cheyenne to the other.

I dozed off right away, but it didn't take. I woke up an hour later with Richie sawing wood in the bed next to me and Johnny off sleeping in the bathtub. I got up and let myself out of the room with as much stealth as I could manage. A blast of warm, wet air slapped me fully awake.

I closed the door and stood for a moment, leaning on the railing, looking down over the small parking lot. A dozen cars and our van filled half the spaces.

I was depressed and I was confused. It didn't make sense. Being on the road should've been the happiest time of my life. This was all I'd ever wanted and I was somehow blowing it. I tried to distract myself by memorizing all the license plates I could read from my perch, but I got bored.

Cheyenne was in the room next to ours and without stopping to think about what I was doing or why, I crept low, sidled up to her door, and listened.

Laughing. No, not laughing. Moaning.

This is the place in the story, FAP, where I expect you will audibly groan, horrified that the protagonist (me) doesn't see what's coming, and that the reader (you) will wonder how such an idiot got to be a protagonist in the first place. But this isn't a story, and I'm not a protagonist. I'm just me. The fact is, sometimes we just don't see what we don't want to see.

Curtains were drawn across the window, but they were being blown out and billowed by the air conditioner, allowing a glimpse inside: A partially finished bottle of Coke sat on a nightstand; a TV screen glowed blue; and Johnny moved to and fro, on top of Cheyenne. I couldn't see their faces, only their bodies from the torso down, but I still knew it was them.

I wanted to throw up, I wanted to bang on the door. At the very least I wanted to walk away. But I could only sit and watch until he was done. Until *they* were done. I let myself back into my room and stretched out in the tub where Johnny was supposed to be.

I shut my eyes and slept the sleep of the dead.

MY BEST FRIEND'S GIRL

(written by Ric Ocasek, and performed by The Cars)

In our junior year of high school, I sat behind Johnny in trigonometry. It was the only time we were ever in the same class.

Johnny McKenna's name was a permanent fixture on the RHS honor roll. He took Advanced Placement courses, aced all his tests, and was on his way to graduating in the top ten of our class. As I've already established it was a different story for me, though there was one exception: math.

There's something about the logic of math that I find beautiful. No, really, I do. It probably has to do with how Dr. Kenny trained me to embrace the truth of things, and math, no matter how you look at it, is always true.

When I got placed into honors trig, my dad was so happy I thought he was going to pee himself. He kept talking about how with math as a foundation I could be an engineer or a physicist. It went in one ear and out the other. I was just psyched that Johnny and I were going to be taking a class together.

For the first few months, it was great. We would meet outside the room, catch each other up on news of the day, and then take our seats. During class, we'd pass notes when the teacher wasn't looking. Johnny always initiated the note passing, usually offering some comment about the band or something he'd seen on TV.

In December of that year, he passed me a note that said: *So are you ever going to get a girlfriend?*

Johnny would say things like this to me all the time. Part of me thinks he was genuinely interested in my happiness. Another part thinks it gave him a feeling of superiority to know that I had no shot. My answer was always the same.

No, I wrote on the note without going into any more detail and passed it back.

Why not?

You know why.

Okay, okay, he wrote back, *but if you WERE going to date a girl, who would you want it to be?*

I didn't really like where this was going, so I put the note in my pocket and didn't answer. A minute later Johnny passed me a new note.

Well????

Well, nothing.

We went back and forth like this for a while, but eventually, Johnny wore me down.

Kristen Greeley, I wrote, sorry I did as soon as the note left my hand. Johnny read it, nodded, and didn't say anymore. I thought that was kind of weird, but then I forgot about it.

Two weeks later, Johnny canceled our nightly run because he had a date with Kristen Greeley. You can draw your own conclusions, FAP, but I think we can both figure out what happened.

The two of them only went out twice. That was enough, I guess, for Johnny to prove his point: namely that he could have everything I couldn't.

And that brings us back to Virginia.

I CAN'T DRIVE 55

(written and performed by Sammy Hagar)

Just before sunrise someone nudged my foot.

It was Johnny.

"Harry?" he asked. I could see right away that he'd figured out why I was sleeping in the tub. He and Cheyenne
were out of the closet. He looked at me, waiting for I don't
know what. Absolution? Celebration? There was nothing
to say, so we just stared at each other for a minute before
he nodded and walked off.

I lay there for a while, not sure what to do. Here are
some of the things I considered:

Broken Heart Remedy #1: Fill the tub with water and
try to drown or maybe electrocute myself. But I didn't
really see how that would help.

Broken Heart Remedy #2: Quit the band and take a bus home, though that didn't seem any better than Remedy #1.

Broken Heart Remedy #3: Get drunk. This was my favorite idea, but it was only five in the morning, and truth be told, I'd only ever been drunk once before and didn't have a fake ID with which to buy booze.

Broken Heart Remedy #4: Punch Johnny in the face and be done with the whole thing. Okay, *this* was my favorite idea, but who was I kidding? I didn't have it in me. Even after watching him break his own promise about Cheyenne, watching him steal the girl I knew should be mine, I still couldn't play any role other than Spock to his Kirk. Strike that. More like Chekov to his Kirk. Strike that again. More like Unnamed Male Ensign Number Three to his Kirk.

Broken Heart Remedy #5 should have been to talk to Johnny and Cheyenne, to clear the air and tell them how I was feeling, but honestly, it never occurred to me.

In the end, I did the only thing I was programmed to do—I pretended it hadn't happened. I buried my emotions in a secret place with no windows and no doors. Either they would suffocate and vanish, or they would catch fire and burn everything down.

Once their relationship was public knowledge, Johnny and Cheyenne flaunted it. They held hands, they hugged and kissed in public, they gave each other little neck massages. Each new sign of affection was like the pinprick of a tiny knife.

I tried to talk to Richie about it, but he just said, "Ah, dude," and walked away. I didn't really know what that meant, but it made me feel kind of stupid, so I didn't ask again.

We had a gig in Durham the next night opening for a popular local band. They were a two-piece—crunchy, rockabilly guitar and spare, taut drums—and they filled the room with students from Duke and UNC. Our music didn't fit the vibe, so we weren't sure how well we'd go over with the crowd, but go over we did. No one told us that our B-side, "Assholes Like Us," had been getting played on the Duke radio station. When we closed our set, half the audience was singing along.

Hey Mom, I'm gonna drop out of school
'Cause I think it's so cool
Gonna play in a rock 'n' roll band.
Don't shed a tear

Was only eighteen years to figure out
You were so bland.

Gonna spend all my money
'Cause I think it's funny
Gonna blow it on a real shitty van

Driving through the states
It'll be great
Getting laid wherever I can.

What's it like to be my mother?
What's it like to be my father?
What's it like to be my brother?
To have to deal with an asshole like me.

Other than big hair and Yuppie bullshit, there didn't seem to be a whole lot to rebel against, so we focused our angst inward, rebelling against ourselves. At least we had a sense of humor about it.

It was by every external measure a great gig, and playing music did let me forget about things for a while. But the sense of relief faded with the last chord of our last song. Watching Johnny and Chey hug one another and laugh after the set was enough to send me into a deep funk. I was in the funk to end all funks. I was Parliament Funkadelic.

When we left the club it was already after three in the morning. There wasn't much point in trying to find a place to sleep, so we decided to drive straight through to our next gig, in Athens, Georgia.

I drove the first shift with Richie next to me in the passenger seat, his mouth open and drooling, his slow breathing keeping time with the whine of the tires on the road. A 7-Eleven Big Gulp full of Coke was balanced on his lap. We had a rule that whoever rode in the passenger seat was supposed to help the driver stay awake and entertained. It only seemed to work when I was the passenger. Johnny and Cheyenne were sacked out in the back, the two of them twisted together like a pretzel.

Every time I caught a glimpse of myself in the rearview mirror, or in the transparent reflection cast by the dashboard lights on the interior of the windshield, I felt sick. I was grotesque, a thing to be shunned, an Untouchable. And that seemed right to me. A person who looked like me didn't have the right to feel anything different, didn't deserve to be happy.

Had I stopped for even just one minute to think about things, had I found a way to step back and gain perspective, I might've felt different. I was the guitar player in a touring rock band and was living every kid's dream. Even more than that, the stage was the one place where my scars didn't matter. Sure, I did my best to cover my face and neck, but people still knew there was something wrong with me—I mean, duh, we were called the Scar Boys for a reason—they just didn't care. To them I was just a guy in a band. A good band. A band that made them want to dance and shout and sing. I, Harbinger Robert Francis Jones, was making people happy. That should've been enough to make me happy, too. But perspective, I'm told, doesn't come easily to teenagers, and it never came to me at all.

I tried to distract the tornado swirling in my head by listing, in alphabetical order, every word I could remember from eleventh grade Spanish, starting with *almuerzo*. I got as far as *desayuno* when a loud metallic rattle, coming from somewhere deep inside the engine, announced itself with a fury.

We were somewhere near Spartanburg, South Carolina.

"What's that noise?" Richie asked, sitting up straight and rubbing his eyes. His sudden movement caused the Big Gulp to spill all over his pants.

"Shit," he muttered. He was half annoyed and half amused. That was what I always loved about Richie. He could find the humor in anything.

The noise in the engine sounded like a handful of ball bearings thrown into a washing machine.

"I don't know what it is," I answered, "it just started. And we seem to be losing power."

"Since when?" he asked.

"Since right now. I have it floored and we're only doing fifty."

"Shit," he said again, tapping his teeth with his fingernail and looking at his watch. "Get off at the next exit."

Five minutes later we found ourselves in the parking lot of a McDonald's, the interior shrouded in darkness, the golden arches silent and gray.

"Stay here and rev the engine when I say so." Richie hopped out and went to a pay phone in front of the van.

Johnny stirred in the back. "What's going on?"

I didn't answer. My anger had become a festering sore that needed to burst, but I wouldn't let it.

"Harry?"

"Something wrong with Dino," I mumbled. "I think Richie wants to call his dad."

"Cotter pin?"

"I have no idea."

Richie motioned to me, so I stepped on the gas, throttling up the volume of the rattle in the engine.

"That doesn't sound good," Johnny said.

"What's he doing?" Cheyenne asked, pointing at Richie.

I couldn't believe it, but Richie was holding the pay phone up to the van. He had me gun the accelerator a few more times, talked for another minute, hung up, and hopped back in. The look on my face must've asked the unstated question.

"I wanted my dad to hear the engine," he said.

"Over a pay phone?"

"You got a better idea?" I didn't. "He says we probably threw an engine rod."

"Let me guess, that's bad," Johnny said.

"Yeah, that's real bad," Richie answered, unable to hide the anxiety in his voice. "If we did throw a rod, it's only a matter of time until the engine stops working all together and needs to be replaced."

"Replace the engine?"

"Yeah."

We were all silent for a moment.

"Is there any—" Johnny started.

"No. I mean, we can put heavier oil in, but that'll only buy us time. Think of this sucker as having a massive brain tumor. The survival rate is zero." As we talked about it more, I learned from Richie that technically, we hadn't "thrown the rod" yet. One of the shafts in the engine that moves the pistons had come loose and was knocking around. That was the rattling. And because we had one piston malfunctioning badly, we didn't have full power. That was the poor acceleration. In time the rod would come completely loose and break through the engine casing. When that happened, we were dead in the water.

"So what do we do?" I asked.

"We keep going for as long as we can." This from Johnny. I looked at Richie who could only shrug.

"Okay then." I put Dino in gear, and pulled back onto the highway.

Twenty-nine miles later, there was a loud THWACK! Thick smoke filled the cabin of the van and oil spewed everywhere on the road. I was able to make it to the shoulder where Dino let out his last gasp and died on the spot. We were still one hundred miles from Athens—all our equipment, all our luggage, all our hopes and dreams entombed in rusted metal.

MORE CIGARETTES

(written by Paul Westerberg, and performed by The Replacements)

Johnny and Cheyenne hoofed it to the next exit, a little more than a mile away, and called a wrecker to have the van towed. The dispatcher told them that the trip to Athens was going to cost two hundred dollars, most of the cash we had left.

None of us could find a single word to say while we waited. It was the first time since I'd known Johnny that he was without some clever remark, without an obvious solution no one else could see. That more than anything else scared the crap out of me.

When the wrecker arrived, I volunteered to ride in the tow truck while the rest of the band rode in the van. Given everything that had happened in the last twenty-four hours, I needed space.

The driver they sent to rescue us was your garden-variety, twenty-something, old-school redneck—denim overalls, blue-checked flannel shirt, scuffed work boots, even a John Deere hat—or so I thought. It turns out you shouldn't judge a book by its cover (you'd think I, of all people, would know that!) because he was actually a stoner from New Jersey.

"Yeah, man, I just came to Athens because I heard UGA was a party school. Want some?" I didn't know how, but this guy had managed to roll a joint while he was driving. According to the speedometer we were doing ninety. He waved the fat boy under my nose.

I guess it's weird, that, at eighteen, playing in a band, and spending most of my adolescence trying to fit in, I hadn't been stoned before. Well, not unless you count being a methadone addict as a fourth grader, which I'm choosing not to count. Anyway, recreational drug use, for whatever reason, had just never come up.

"Yeah, okay," I said.

The driver, whose name was Jeremiah, lit the joint, sucked the sweet smelling smoke deep into his chest, and held his breath. Then he passed it to me. I tried to mimic what I saw, but wound up in a fit of coughing and sputtering. As I tried to refill my lungs with fresh air, the coughing morphed into a kind of maniacal laughter that ended as teary gasps for breath. Jeremiah laughed, too, but I think it was just to be polite.

Only three years older than me, Jeremiah (not "Jerry" I was told) had recently dropped out of UGA and taken a job with Northern Georgia Wreck & Rescue, the company with the exclusive contract to handle calls to the state police along I-85. He'd been studying psychology, but that was just to please his parents. Jeremiah's true love was driving, fixing, and being around cars. He spent his week-ends at the Dixie Speedway in Woodstock, just north of Atlanta, working a stock car crew and hoping for a chance to race.

"So what's wrong with your van, anyway?" he asked.

"We threw an engine rod."

"Oh, you boys are fucked." He took another long toke and handed the joint back to me. By my third drag I was smoking without convulsing, though to be honest, I didn't feel any different. I thought being stoned would make me light-headed and happy. I just felt nauseous and my throat burned.

I handed what was left of the joint back to Jeremiah who carefully stubbed it out on the steering wheel, add-ing another burn mark to the twenty or thirty that were already in orbit around the truck's horn. He dropped the roach in his shirt pocket and then pulled out a pack of Marlboro's, offering it in my direction.

"Sure," I said, "why not."

I flicked the lighter and held the thin orange flame to

the end of the cigarette until I saw it was burning and then drew the smoke in. The taste of tobacco was foul compared to pot. It was like the difference between coffee and coffee ice cream. I held the soupy fog in my lungs for a long moment and exhaled.

"No, no, no, son." Jeremiah laughed. "You exhale these right away. Don't you smoke?"

"Not until today."

"What the hell you wanna start for now?"

I didn't have a good answer, so I shrugged my shoulders and took another drag, doing it right the second time. The truth is, I didn't care why. I just wanted to smoke. Sue me.

The conversation petered out and we rode in silence for a while. Then Jeremiah asked, "So is Harry short for Harold?"

As you can probably guess, I hate that question. It comes up way more than you would think. But my name is my name, so I answered.

"No, it's Harbinger."

"Harbinger?"

"Yeah."

"Like Harbinger of Doom?" Jeremiah was both amused and perplexed.

Maybe it was the pot, maybe it was the nicotine, but something loosened me up enough that I found myself telling Jeremiah the whole sorry story of how I got my name. It goes something like this:

My parents met in September 1967, which was supposed to be the "Summer of Love."

Race riots were flaring in a dozen cities, the Chinese were exploding H-bombs in the Gobi Desert, and the US Congress was upping the ante in Vietnam, turning a police action into a full-fledged war. Summer of Love? It was more like the summer of indigestion, like 1966 had eaten a bad taco and just couldn't keep it down.

My mom was working nights at a diner in Brooklyn to put herself through Kingsborough Community College, when my dad stopped in for a cup of coffee. He had been in Prospect Park for an event with his boss, Senator Robert Francis Kennedy; yeah, *that* Kennedy. Dad's first political job was as a junior staffer, a constituent liaison or something like that, for the one and only Bobby Kennedy.

Dad sat at the counter of the diner and flirted with my mom for an hour. (She says it was more like two hours.) When he finally introduced himself and she shook his hand, there was an electric shock so intense that all the lights went out. Literally. All five boroughs of New York City went dark in a blackout that lasted five hours.

Halfway through that blackout I was conceived, and three weeks later my parents were married.

Yeah, I know, gross.

Things started off really good for my mom and dad. They bought a small house in Yonkers and began to build a life.

Then, in March of 1968, Kennedy jumped into the presidential race. My dad was offered a job on the campaign team, so he wound up traveling with the senator. It was hard on my mom, but the payoff if Kennedy won—and everyone was pretty sure he would win—was a job for my dad and an exciting new life in Washington for the Jones family.

Mom went into labor in the early hours of the morning on June 5. Her first contraction began at the exact same moment an unemployed exercise rider from Santa Anita racetrack was squeezing the trigger that would put a bullet into Bobby Kennedy's head. My father was just a few yards away when it happened. (The gunshot, not the contraction.)

Dad talks about that night often, his eyes glazing over, his voice going hoarse, like he's still there, stuck in that moment. He pulls out the same photograph of Kennedy and his entourage onstage at the Ambassador Hotel in Los Angeles, all of them smiling with their arms raised in celebration at having just won the California primary.

"See that ear?" my father asks, pointing to the obscured view of a man's head, five people deep on the stage. "That's my ear.

"Bobby," Dad tells me, "was heading for a press conference after his victory speech. That's when I heard the shots and I knew they got him. I knew they got Bobby."

At this point my father usually stops and stares at his hands. I can never tell if he's really getting emotional, or if he's just pausing for effect. Then he takes a deep breath and starts again.

"The next thing I knew, I was waking up in a hospital room with a big lump on my head. I don't remember how I got there or how I got hurt. Something must have happened in the chaos after the shooting. When word reached me that your mother had gone into labor, I was confused— I had a concussion, and was probably still in shock—but I knew that I had to get home."

Thirty hours later, the story goes, when he finally made it to my mother's bedside, dazed and smelling like stale cigarettes and taxicab air freshener, my dad could barely hold me.

"Ben," my mother said as my father gazed into my half-shut eyes for the first time, "he still needs a name."

Not yet ready to move on from the grief and confusion he'd left behind in California to the joy of new life, my father could only mutter, "Harbinger."

My mother, a puzzle of a woman if ever there was one, smiled and said, "Okay, Harbinger Robert Francis Jones."

The events of those agonizing two days finally caught up with my dad, and he broke down. He climbed into the hospital bed next to my mom. With me cradled between them, and with my mother stroking his hair, my father cried himself to sleep.

Dad could never bring himself to call me Bobby like my mother wanted, so they started calling me Harry instead, and it stuck.

But it's hard to escape a name like Harbinger. And, of course they had no idea what a good choice it would turn out to be.

When I finished the story Jeremiah just looked at me and gave a long low whistle.

"That is one fucked-up story, Harbinger Jones."

We didn't say much else after that, and a few minutes later Jeremiah found the Athens address I'd given him— a low ranch house with light blue siding on a sleepy street. We'd been steered here by the drummer from the Woofing Cookies. This was the house of a friend of a friend, and arrangements had been made to let us crash for a few days. Jeremiah left Dino at the end of the driveway.

When I went to shake his hand, he was holding out his pack of Marlboros; inside was the roach from earlier. He winked at me and said, "Take care Harbinger Robert Francis Jones. Stay out of trouble." And with that, he was gone.

I WANNA BE SEDATED

(written by Joey Ramone, and performed by the Ramones)

I woke up in a pitch-black room, sweating and out of breath. I was having a nightmare and must've been making some sort of horrible noise because Johnny came bursting through the door to see what was wrong.

"I'm all right," I started to say, "it was just . . ." But Johnny didn't stop at the door. He bounded into the room, leapt onto my chest, and wrapped his hands around my throat, choking all the air out of my lungs.

My heart seized and I fell out of bed, waking up for real.

Richie was on the floor next to me, sprawled like a chalk outline. His snoring didn't even break its rhythm when I hit the ground.

There was light spilling under the door and I heard muffled voices on the other side. Johnny and Cheyenne. They were talking low and laughing.

I caught my breath and got my bearings—we were still in Athens, still crashing in the same house. The room had no air conditioner and my shirt was soaked through.

I got up, grabbed my cigarettes, and snuck out.

Johnny and Cheyenne were in their own room with the door closed. The light I saw was coming from a kitchen, where a stove clock read 3:24. I walked past the refrigerator, out the back door, and lit a smoke.

Off to the right, difficult to make out in the dark, was a twelve foot half-pipe made of pine boards and two-by-fours. It had been built by Tony and Chuck, the two skate punks who lived in the house. Shaved heads, piercings, and tattoos notwithstanding, they were actually pretty nice guys. Despite the fashion choice, they had more in common with Jeff Spicoli than with Aryan youth. All they wanted to do was ride that pipe and drink beer.

Dino was parked in the driveway to my left, wearing his name like a badge of honor. Our van had become a dinosaur, a reminder of another age. Useless and extinct, it had been sitting idle since we arrived two days earlier.

Our first morning in Athens we'd found the local Ford dealer and learned it was going to cost seventeen hundred dollars to fix the van. The entire engine block needed to be replaced. We didn't have the money, and none of us were willing to ask our families for a loan, so we began canceling tour dates. It felt a little like quitting methadone, but with no reward at the end. Each gig lost was a punch in the gut. We canceled four dates the first day, and another two the second. We gave ourselves one week to get it sorted out and get back on the road. No one talked about what would happen at the end of that week.

I used the embers of my dying cigarette to light another and decided to go for a walk.

I started off at a rapid clip, the slap of my sneakers against the pavement sounding like the heartbeat of a small bird. I tried to get my mind around everything that was happening—the van, the tour, Johnny and Cheyenne— but it was all too much, so I started listing world capitals instead.

Abu Dhabi, Accra, Addis Ababa.

The air was a stew of humidity and heat, the only breeze generated by my own movement. The farther I walked, the faster I walked, but it did nothing to cool me off.

Algiers, Amman, Amsterdam.

I couldn't slow down, body or mind.

Once, when I was nine or ten years old, I was in the car with my mother going to some doctor or other when the gas pedal got stuck. Bad things always seemed to happen when my mother was behind the wheel of a car. In this case, a little metal burr on the accelerator caught on an adjoining piece of metal in the engine and opened an uninterrupted and unquenchable flow of gasoline to the pistons. The brakes, when fully engaged, produced acrid-smelling smoke but did nothing to slow our speed. The car couldn't be stopped. That's how I felt walking through that stifling night, like that car careening out of control. (My mom eventually saved us by putting the car in neutral and coasting to safety. Unfortunately, I didn't seem to have a neutral gear. Only drive and reverse.)

Andorra la Vella, Ankara, Antananarivo.

The mantra of the capitals was the only tangible thing in the world. The only thing I could hold on to. I was seeing everything as if reflected in a room of fun-house mirrors—distorted, ugly, unreal—and I couldn't find my way out. Parked cars looked like something from an Escher print and the trees were melting. Either the world was breaking down or I was.

Asunción, Athens, Baghdad.

I had no idea where my feet were taking me, so I was surprised when I rounded a corner and found myself in the center of town. Without knowing how or why, I made a beeline for the pay phone outside of the Athens police station and dialed the first and only number that popped into my brain.

"Dr. Hirschorn's line," said a bored woman's voice. For some stupid reason, I'd imagined that Dr. Kenny would answer the phone himself. It never occurred to me that doctors didn't answer their own phones, especially in the middle of the night.

"I have a collect call from a Harry Jones," the operator answered.

There was a pause on the other end of the line. Apparently the answering service lady hadn't encountered collect calls before. Not sure what to do, she accepted the charges.

"May I help you?" she asked, her boredom replaced by alarm.

"I need to speak to Dr. Kenny," I managed to rasp into the receiver.

"Dr. Kenny?"

"Dr. Hirschorn."

"Is this an emergency?"

"No. I'm calling in the middle of the night, collect, and can barely breathe. Of course it's an emergency! Do you think I want to sell him a set of encyclopedias?" Even if I had said that, the poor woman on the other end of the line wouldn't have understood a word of it. But I didn't say that or anything intelligible. I don't think I was capable of forming actual sentences.

"Sir?" she asked.

My only response was to continue blathering world capitals in between gasps of weeping.

"Hold, please," she said somewhere around *Beirut*.

I had stopped seeing Dr. Kenny not long after Johnny and I started the band. It was my idea to end our sessions. Dr. Kenny resisted.

"What you've been through, Harry," he'd told me, "it's a lot more complicated than it seems. It's wonderful that you've made friends and are playing music, but there's healing that needs to happen at a deeper level, too. And that takes time."

I'd already been through six years of sessions with Dr. Kenny, and I was having none of it. The only thing I'd ever wanted was a normal life, and there was no place for a pediatric psychiatrist in the world I was trying to build. My parents—my mom still indulging my every desire and my dad wanting to save money—took my side.

Dr. Kenny seemed genuinely worried at our last session.

"Well, the music will be good therapy, I guess," he told me, and he turned out to be right. "You take care, Harbinger Jones," he said as I left his office for the last time.

I did have some regret, not because I thought I needed therapy—though, of course I did—but because I really liked and trusted Dr. Kenny. It's why I was calling him and not my parents from that phone booth in Athens.

Just after *Lima* and right before *Lisbon* Dr. Kenny came on the line.

"Harry, is that you?" he asked, as I continued to gasp for air.

"Yes."

"It's been a while, Harry." Dr. Kenny dropped his voice a cool octave. It was one of his Jedi mind tricks, and it worked. A *this-isn't-the-anxiety-you're-looking-for* sort of thing. "Can you tell me what's happening?"

I didn't know where to begin. My brain fumbled through the facts of my life, groping for a starting point, but found none.

"Harry, it will help if you talk to me."

I saw my reflection in the glass of the phone booth and I froze.

Throughout the course of my life, I'd had one of two reactions on seeing myself in a mirror:

Reflection Reaction #1: Complete revulsion. I was as horrified at my face as everyone around me. I was a scary-looking freak. I got it.

Reflection Reaction #2: The mental airbrush. On the very rare occasions when I wasn't feeling desperate, despondent, detached, or any other SAT word that starts with the letter "d," I would see myself as I imagined I would've looked without the scars, without the nerve damage, without the wig. I would see an unremarkable face—beautiful in its unremarkability, if that's even a word. I would see in my reflection a normal kid.

But something different happened in the phone booth that night. For reasons I didn't understand then and don't understand now, rather than scare me, my face—with all of its horror intact—was, for the first time in my life, a comfort. Maybe I had become so emotionally isolated that I had no one left to turn to other than myself. Or maybe I just didn't care anymore. Whatever the reason, my reflection gave me a glimmer of stability. The phone call to Dr. Kenny started to feel like a bad idea.

"Nothing," I mumbled, "I'm okay. I'm sorry to have bothered you."

"Harry, wait," Dr. Kenny said before I could hang up. I didn't answer, but I knew he could hear me breathing. "I want you to listen to me carefully. You need to get yourself to an emergency room. Can you do that? For me?"

I didn't answer again. My heart rate was starting to retreat from the redline. Barely, but noticeably, I was starting to feel the ground beneath my feet again.

"Harry?"

"No, really doc. I'm going to be okay. And I am sorry to have bothered you. Thank you." I hung up and stood there for a few minutes with my forehead pressed against the glass, letting its smooth surface cool me. I remember that I laughed out loud, but I don't remember why. Had someone been passing by, I'm sure I would've sounded batshit crazy. Lucky for me, the street was deserted.

I left the phone booth and began the long walk back.

SITTING STILL

(written by Bill Berry, Peter Buck, Mike Mills, Michael Stipe, and performed by R.E.M.)

When I got back to the skate house, I found Cheyenne sitting on the back stoop. Her legs were pulled up tight against her chest and she was rocking back and forth with the precision of a metronome. She didn't say anything or even look up when I approached.

"Hey," I muttered, ready to scoot around her and retreat inside. I was still shaky from my walk and phone call, and felt like maybe I should be alone. But when I passed her, I could hear that Cheyenne was crying. The sound stopped me in my tracks.

I didn't know what to do. A crying girl wasn't anything I'd encountered before.

Wait, strike that.

Dana Dimarco.

I was eleven years old and had been walking home across the otherwise deserted elementary school playground. Dana was there, sitting on a swing, dragging her foot in a small, slow circle on the asphalt. She was sobbing openly.

I had stayed late after school that day to avoid a bully named Jamie Cosite. He was a year younger than me and was planning to beat me up. I knew this because during playtime on the kickball field he told me, "I'm going to beat you up."

Going against my better judgment I asked him, "Why?"

"Whaddya mean why?"

"I mean why do you want to beat me up?" I had been so routinely abused by other kids that I guess on some level, I figured I had nothing to lose.

"Because look at you," he said, his friends laughing at his oh-so-clever wit. Cosite had too many freckles and an unnaturally square jaw; he looked like a ventriloquist dummy.

"So?"

That was all he needed. He punched me in the face right then and there, and kicked me in the shoulder as I went down. A teacher saw the commotion and walked straight over to where we were standing. Jamie stopped the assault when he saw her coming toward us, but managed to get in a quick "I'll finish you after school," before the teacher's presence sent all the other kids scattering.

Miss Chardette—"Bulldog Chardette"—the warden of

my sixth-grade class, stood over me. I was alone, lying there on the ground, looking up at her, silently pleading for help. She just shook her head and walked away.

That was the last time I talked back to a bully.

When the last bell rang that day, going outside seemed like a bad idea, so I hid in a coat closet. This was right after Dr. Kenny had first taught me to use lists as calming devices. I began with the only one other than lightning that I'd memorized to that point: US presidents. I ran through the list forward and backward. I counted the even-numbered presidents, and then the odd-numbered presidents. I figured out that the most common letter of the alphabet to begin a president's last name was "H"—Harrison, Hayes, Harrison, Harding, and Hoover—and that only one president's last name began with the letter "L"—Lincoln. The exercise must've worked, because I fell asleep.

When I woke up and dragged myself out of the closet, the clock on the wall of the classroom said it was four p.m. The school was deserted. That's when I went outside and found Dana Dimarco crying on the swings.

As I walked by, she looked out from underneath her copper bangs. She didn't say anything, but I know she saw me. She cast her eyes back to the ground and started crying louder.

I figured I had two choices:

Choice #1: Sit down on the next swing over and ask her what was wrong. Experience taught me that would only lead to disaster. I would do something—or rather, I *was* something—that would make her cry harder.

Choice #2: Walk away.

I chose door number two, and I've regretted it every day of my life since.

If I had talked to Dana Dimarco, maybe I would've made a friend. Truth is, she wasn't totally awful to me most of the time. I bet if I had bothered to ask her what was wrong—and I think she *wanted* me to ask—maybe my whole life would've been different.

I sat down next to Cheyenne, leaving a healthy buffer between us. She didn't say a word, but she didn't have to; something in the air told me that being there was the right thing to do. She needed company.

I don't know how long we sat there—the two of us on that stoop, saying nothing—but the sky turned from the color of a plum, to the color of faded blue jeans, to dawn, and Chey had stopped crying. I'd almost forgotten she was next to me. I was just starting to hatch this crazy idea that we should steal a van to finish the tour when Chey cleared her throat and brought me back to reality.

I turned to face her. She must have sensed that she had my attention because she didn't look up before she spoke.

"We had a big fight." Her voice was flat, matter-of-fact. I didn't have to ask who *we* was. I knew who *we* was.

"Oh." I didn't know what to say next, so I said nothing.

Chey plowed on, not realizing that I was the last person on the planet who wanted to hear about her problems with Johnny. "He wants us to leave, to go home. I told him we all agreed to wait until the end of the week, but he says he doesn't care, he wants to leave now and I should go with him."

"Mmm-hmm," I said.

I know what you're thinking. This was my chance to pile on Johnny, drive a wedge between him and Cheyenne, but honestly, I didn't have it in me.

"He has money, you know." This caught my attention.

"No, I didn't know."

"Yep."

"How much?"

"Like five hundred dollars. His parents gave it to him for emergencies. *Chey,*" she said, mocking Johnny's voice, *"if this isn't an emergency, I don't know what is."*

Johnny had money? He and Chey were fighting? I didn't know what to do. I'd only just barely pulled myself back from the edge of a breakdown and I felt empty, hollowed out, like someone had removed all of my internal organs and replaced them with bags full of sand. Nothing in me was real.

Chey started to cry again, which was the only sound in the world less bearable than the silence.

"What are you going to do?" I asked.

"What do you mean?"

"Are you going with him?"

"To do what?" she said, unable or unwilling to sniffle the edge out of her voice. "Spend a week following him around until he leaves for Syracuse? Then what? Follow him there? He begged me to go, but I don't see the point."

"Johnny begged you to go?" I couldn't picture Johnny begging anyone for anything.

"I guess that's not the right word. He kinda ordered me to go. That's what started the fight."

I nodded. Something about Johnny ordering Chey to go with him reminded me of my father, maybe because it had the unmistakable ring of moral superiority. It never occurred to either one of them—Johnny or my dad—that they could possibly be wrong, about anything, ever.

Case in point: Once, a few years earlier, Johnny told me that he'd heard "they" were breeding six-legged chickens.

"Huh?" I responded.

"Yeah, I saw it on a TV show. They want to sell more drumsticks." Johnny was always bringing some crazy bit of information like that to our rehearsals:

"They're using coffee enemas to cure cancer."

"A nail punch will shatter your car's windshield if you ever drive into a lake."

"Carrie Fisher is really a dude."

Crazy as these tidbits sounded, this was Johnny, so I just accepted whatever he said as true. The chicken thing though, sounded just a bit too crazy, so I put up a meager and casual resistance, which for me was a lot.

"C'mon," I said, "that can't be for real."

Johnny was flabbergasted. You could almost hear him thinking, *How dare you talk back.*

He quoted every detail he could remember from the television show—except its name—and kept pushing, not letting us rehearse until I said I believed him. I never did. I finally shrugged my shoulders, thinking the whole thing was funny, and that the incident was over. But Johnny was so hell-bent on proving his point—just like my dad would've been in the same situation—that he actually wrote a letter to Frank Perdue for validation. Really. Frank Perdue. I kid you not. As far as I know, the letter went unanswered.

When I think about it now, I wonder if Johnny wasn't some sort of surrogate for my dad. Freaky. And beside the point.

"I don't know what to do, Harry," Chey said. It was more or less an open plea for help, but I had nothing. I wanted to help Cheyenne—more than anything in the world I wanted to help Cheyenne—but I couldn't even help myself.

The last time I'd felt this way was the afternoon I'd been rejected by Gabrielle. That day Johnny was there to pick me up. "We should start a band," he'd said. It was like a magic phrase—abracadabra, hocus pocus, and open sesame all rolled into one. It made me forget the pain for just long enough to move on to the next thing.

Sitting there with Chey, I wished for that magic phrase again. Strike that. Not for the phrase, but for how it made me feel, full of wonder and promise. I wished I had bottled that feeling, let it age, and uncorked it there on that porch.

And that's when it hit me. The only thing in the world that could ever make anyone feel truly better.

"I have an idea," I said, "that will help us both." I reached out my hand for Chey. This was so unlike me—taking action and initiative, being direct—that I'm not sure she knew what to do. After a moment she put her hand in mine and let me help her up.

"Let's go."

HIT ME WITH YOUR BEST SHOT

(written by Eddie Schwartz, and performed by Pat Benatar)

During our first sixty hours in Athens, we'd done the following:

Athens Thing #1: We found the mechanic and got the bad news about Dino.

Athens Thing #2: We listened to Johnny whine that we needed to give up the tour and go home.

Athens Thing #3: We waited outside the downtown phone booth while Johnny called his parents and told them that the van had broken down and that we were stranded. He made them promise to be in touch with everyone else's family. They made him promise to call again the next day.

Athens Thing #2: We listened to Johnny whine that we needed to give up the tour and go home.

Athens Thing #4: We watched Richie try his hand at skateboarding. With his arms flailing and whirling, he managed to stay afloat all the way into the trough of the half-pipe, but as the momentum carried the board up the opposite slope, he fell backward and landed hard on his ass. It took him a minute to realize he was okay, and when he did, he raised both arms and yelled, "Fucking A!" in triumph. Tony, Chuck, and the other skate punks shrieked with delight.

Athens Thing #2: We listened to Johnny whine that we needed to give up the tour and go home.

Athens Thing #5: We explored downtown Athens. We found a secondhand record store (we had no money so we browsed), a local sub shop called Judy's (where we learned that subs were called "po'boys"), and the University of Georgia campus (where a steady stream of unpleasant looks suggested we were less than welcome).

Athens Thing #2: We listened to Johnny whine that we needed to give up the tour and go home.

Athens Thing #6: And we—meaning me—read a book in the living room while Johnny and Cheyenne sat on the front porch swing and made out. (Not true. I pretended to read a book while I spied on Johnny and Cheyenne through the venetian blinds.)

Those were the things we'd done after crash-landing in Athens. Here's what we hadn't done:

Athens Thing #0: Play music.

Cheyenne followed me inside, and I led her straight to her bass. "Here," I said, "I'll get the other guys."

Cheyenne smiled. "Good idea. Where?"

"Richie set his drums up in the basement."

The basement of the skate house was a strange space. There were four rooms, each separated from the others by brick walls, all but one with a hard-packed dirt floor. There were odd pieces of furniture scattered about, including a giant cherry wood dresser, a rolltop desk, and a toilet, which for some reason cracked Richie up.

The other things of note in the basement were the jumping spiders.

I don't know if they were technically spiders because I'd never seen anything like them before, and haven't seen anything like them since. In fact, I'm not entirely sure they were of this world. They were dime-sized bugs that hopped vertically in the air, moving with precision and menace. A group of them together looked like the tiny pistons of a tiny car engine. (Notice that I didn't say *van* engine because as you now know, FAP, *van engines* do not work.) There were hundreds of the little monstrosities. They were mostly restricted to a back corner of the basement, which left the rest of the space safe for human habitation. Every so often one of the spiders would venture into the green zone, which made it fair game. The only house rule Tony and Chuck had was to never go into the basement in bare feet.

I kicked Richie's foot as I walked into our shared bedroom, waking him up. He made an unintelligible sound, a breathy amalgam of "what" and "fuck," and looked at me. "Jesus, Harry, what time is it?"

"I don't know. Six or seven maybe?"

"Is the house on fire?"

"No."

"Then piss off."

"We're jamming."

Richie's eyes opened all the way and he smiled. He got up and grabbed his drumsticks and pants, in that order, and headed downstairs.

Johnny was in the room he and Cheyenne had been sharing, sitting on the edge of the bed, staring at his fully packed knapsack.

"I told you guys I was going to college," he said to me as soon as I crossed the threshold, defending himself before I could say a word.

"C'mon," I told him, waving him to follow me.

"Where?"

"We're jamming."

"Harry, I think I need to leave." Johnny sounded exasperated, defeated.

"I know," I said, looking at my shoes. "Cheyenne told me. But why don't you come jam first?"

"What? Why?"

"I dunno." It was a coward's answer. The truth was that he should come jam because he was my best friend and music was the only thing left holding us together. That whatever he and I had once meant to each other was seeping away like water from a drought-stricken lake, too slowly to be noticed, until one day it would just be gone. That even if he was going to leave, he should go out, literally, on a high note. But I wasn't programmed to say those things. I wanted to, but didn't know how.

"If you don't know, then I sure don't know," he answered. His voice had an edge and a meanness that hurt, and I reacted.

"Cheyenne says you have money," I said. It felt good to catch him in a lie, to force him to the moral low ground.

Silence.

I looked up at Johnny and met his eyes. It's important

to understand that I'd never said anything so directly con-
frontational in the entire history of our friendship. This
was new ground for both of us.

"It's none of your business," he finally answered.

"It's not?"

"No."

"You didn't seem to mind spending the money my dad
gave me."

"That was your choice, Harry. Besides, my parents told
me this was emergency money."

"And the van breaking down? That wasn't an emergency?"

"My emergency, not your emergency. And like I said, it's
none of your business." He was defiant, smug and secure
in the rightness of his actions to the last. I couldn't take it.

"Asshole." I muttered the word under my breath. It was
dripping with malice, and it was out of my mouth before I
could stop it.

Johnny's eyebrows arched so sharply in surprise that they
looked like two garden slugs trying to crawl off his forehead
and into his hair. "I'm sorry, did you say something?"

My utterance of "asshole" was so far off the script of
our well-defined relationship that I knew I'd crossed a line
and it scared me. I shook my head no.

He stared right through me and with all the cruelty he
could muster, said, "You. Are. Such. A. Pussy." And then
he smiled.

When I think about it now, I know that Johnny was

feeling the same stress, or at least his own version of the stress, that the rest of us were feeling. And when I think about it now, I know that Johnny's best defense has always been a good offense. But that's only if I think about it now. In the heat of that moment, something in me snapped. It was like when the cotter pin on Dino snapped; the clutch was still there, and the gears were still there, but any connection between the two was gone. I had no control. Strike that. In some weird way, I think I had total control. I'd switched to autopilot. All feeling and all thought peeled away from me like a snake's skin molting.

Maybe I snapped because I hadn't slept. Or maybe it was a hangover from the flood of emotions I'd experienced the night before. Or maybe it was the years of abuse and neglect, the cruelty upon cruelty inflicted on me. Or maybe it was that Johnny had broken the promise we'd all made not to date Cheyenne, ever, and that he did it before I'd had the chance. Maybe it was all of those things, or maybe it was something else entirely. But when I look back, I think it was his smile that pushed me over the edge.

Time froze. I saw everything as a collection of brightly glowing pixels, each point of light so intense I couldn't look straight at it, but all the pixels together rendering the world in perfect, stark clarity, as if illuminated by a pro-longed flash of lightning. Every nerve ending in my body was humming. Strike that. Not humming, thrumming, like what you feel if you're standing too close to high voltage power lines. I was either going to float away or explode.

I didn't float away.

I dropped my arms to my sides and looked Johnny in the eye. He didn't flinch. My right hand opened itself into a flat paddle, and with all my might, my arm swung out wide and slapped Johnny in the face. I hit him hard enough that his head swiveled to the side and his cheek turned red.

He looked back at me stunned. "Did you just slap me?"

I turned and walked out of the room.

PUMP IT UP

(written and performed by Elvis Costello)

"Where's Johnny?" Chey asked without looking up. She was sitting on the edge of her amp tuning her bass.

"Upstairs," I answered as I plugged my guitar in.

After my open-handed slap I made straight for the basement. I saw Chey and Richie exchange a glance as I pulled the guitar strap over my head. They could tell something was wrong.

You're probably thinking that I was feeling one of the following emotions in that moment:

Anger.

Joy.

Relief.

Fear.

Guilt.

Sorrow.

The truth is, more than anything, I was embarrassed. Embarrassed that I'd slapped Johnny and not punched him in the face. When someone calls you a pussy, an open-handed slap only proves his point. That's what I was thinking when I went downstairs. The whole episode showed how damaged my friendship with Johnny was. I didn't know if he would come down the stairs or not, and by then, I really didn't care. I just wanted to move on.

"Let's play a song," I said.

"Is he coming?" Cheyenne asked, looking worried.

As if on cue, the sound of stomping footsteps upstairs made the ceiling shake. We all stopped—me standing and holding my guitar, Richie sitting behind his drums, and Chey perched on the edge of her amp—and waited. Then we heard the front door of the house open and slam shut.

No one moved for a least a full minute, probably more like two.

Cheyenne broke the silence. I don't know what was going through her head. She probably thought Johnny had left because of her. She set her jaw in the locked position and started playing the bass line to our nastiest, fastest song.

Playing loud, hard music was the tonic I needed. Strike that. Johnny leaving was the tonic I needed. Strike that, too. It wasn't just one thing, it was everything. It was hitting bottom the night before, it was connecting with Cheyenne on the stoop, it was the music, it was confronting Johnny, it was all of it. I—we—played like the world was going to end in five minutes and this was the last thing any of us would ever get to do.

I was the only one who knew the words to all our songs (I had memorized them), so with Johnny gone, I set up his microphone and sang. And you know what? I was good. Really good. I could see it in Richie's and Chey's faces. I was surprising them as much as I was surprising myself. I wasn't even wearing my costume.

We got through a whole forty-five minutes before the police showed up. We didn't hear them until they were coming down the stairs. There were two officers—both young, both built like football players—and they looked kind of amused.

We stopped playing.

"Do you kids know what time it is?" the taller of the two asked.

"Isn't it like ten a.m.?" Cheyenne asked. I was pretty sure she knew it wasn't, but Chey was a pro at bending the truth.

"No, it's like 7:45 a.m.," he answered, mocking her.

"Huh," Chey said. "I guess we should stop."

I had been in a corner of the cramped, poorly lit room, and had kept my head down. Something about the way I was sitting must've bothered the cop.

"Hey, are you all right?" he asked.

I lifted my head and met his eyes. He tried to check his

reaction, but I could see him recoil. It made me smile. I've always known that I have no ability to control that reaction, to stop the revulsion at the mere sight of me. But for the first time in my life, it didn't bother me. It was what it was; it really didn't matter. It seemed so obvious that I wondered how I'd been missing it all those years.

I thought back to what Lucky Strike the Lightning Man told me, that I had to control things or they would control me. I'd been putting the emphasis on controlling rather than on not being controlled. And maybe that was upside down. Maybe I just needed to figure out how to go with the flow.

"I'm okay," I answered him.

"Okay," he said. "Just cool it with the music until later in the day. We had three complaints."

"Sure thing, officer," Chey said. "Sorry to have brought you out here."

He nodded, said, "Let's go" to his partner, and they left.

"Should we play another song?" Richie asked after we heard their car pull away, the corners of his mouth stretched wide with mischief.

Chey—who looked like she was coming back to Earth, like the feeling of the music was leaving her, like she was remembering that Johnny was gone—shook her head no. "Probably not the best idea. But let's come back later. I really needed this."

"Amen," I said.

When we went upstairs, we found Tony and Chuck in the kitchen drinking coffee and smoking cigarettes.

"Crap," I said. We hadn't even stopped to consider that our hosts were still sleeping. "I'm really sorry if we woke you guys up."

"Are you kidding, man?" Chuck began. "We loved it! We had no idea you guys were that good."

"Really?" Richie asked. He was beaming, and I think I was, too.

"Where's the other dude?" Tony asked.

"Gone," I said. "Home. College."

"Well, fuck him then. You dudes should finish your tour."

The three of us exchanged a glance and I burst out laughing. "We'd love to," I answered, "but we can't afford to fix our van."

"So buy a smaller car. There are always crap cars for sale just outside of town for like five hundred dollars. We can drive you out there."

"Well, five hundred dollars is less than the seventeen hundred it's gonna cost to fix the van, but it doesn't matter, because we barely have fifty dollars between us."

Tony and Chuck looked at each other and said in unison, "Fund-raiser."

HALLELUJAH

(written and performed by Leonard Cohen)

The fund-raiser turned out to be a keg party. A big keg party. A really, really big keg party.

Tony and Chuck made crude signs and enlisted the help of their friends to post them all over town:

> *Help the Scar Boys finish their tour. Rock and roll fund-raiser at 810 Hill Street this Friday* (three nights hence). *$10 to get in, larger donations accepted. Live music, cold brew, and riding the pipe. We start tapping the keg at 9 p.m. Spread the word.*

From what they told us, the fund-raiser was the only thing anyone was talking about. Athens was like that. It was a small town and word spread fast, especially when it involved beer. There were no formal invitations, there was no arm twisting, just the grapevine. This party was, according to Tony and Chuck, going to be huge.

Like always, I stayed away from other people, so I had no idea if they were blowing smoke or not, but I figured not, and I started to freak myself out.

This was going to be the first time we played in public without Johnny, and the first time I would be singing in front of other people. I had no idea what to do, or worse, what to expect of myself.

On the afternoon of the fund-raiser I wandered around the house waiting for the sun to go down. I was trying to kill time, but I think it was killing me instead.

I finished an unfinished crossword puzzle.

I watched *Mayberry R.F.D.* on the television in Tony's room.

I took two walks around the block, counting the individual cement squares on the sidewalk (567).

I even washed the dishes.

I ran out of things to do and wound up on the back porch chain-smoking, staring at the empty pipe and the crude stage we'd built in front of it, and going over the set list in my head, again and again and again.

The sun was low over the horizon, throwing tangerine soup at a herd of passing clouds, when I heard the door close behind me. I was so lost in my own thoughts that I didn't realize it was Cheyenne until she was sitting next to me.

"Hi," she said.

"Hi," I answered.

She seemed to collect her thoughts for a moment and then said, "This doesn't feel right."

"What?"

"Playing this party without Johnny. Finishing the tour without Johnny. Being here, without Johnny."

Since the police had stopped our jam session three mornings earlier, Chey had kept mostly to herself. She stayed in her room, only coming out when we gave her updates on the plans for the fund-raiser, or to rehearse.

"So what do you want to do?" I asked, trying to be gentle. "Do you want to go home?"

"No," she said, "but it still doesn't feel right."

"I think we sound pretty good as a trio," I offered.

"We do." She kind of smiled. "Somehow that makes it worse."

"Look, Chey, if you want to go, we'll all go. We'll do whatever you want to do."

She took my hand and I squeezed her fingers, maybe a little too hard. The next thing I knew, she was kissing my mangled cheek. Her lips were soft. Softer than her hands. Softer than anything in the world. They were the most wonderful things I'd ever felt in my life.

"Thank you, Harry," she said.

"For what?"

"For still being here."

Without thinking about what I was doing, I put my hand on her shoulder and gave her neck a little squeeze. I could feel her muscles release all of their tension, like they just needed human contact. She turned her face to mine.

"Cheyenne . . ." was all I could muster. Our faces were so close that it was mostly an accident when our lips touched. Both of us had our eyes open, and we both froze. Then she closed her eyes and kissed me.

I didn't know what to do. Literally. Was I supposed to pucker up? Press my mouth forward? Open it? Jam my tongue in there? Luckily, kissing is one of those animal instincts I guess we all have, because before I knew what was happening, I was kissing her back—innocent middle-school kisses, gentle, PG-rated kisses.

I would later learn—researching it, like Dr. Kenny taught me to do—that in those few seconds I was kissing Cheyenne, more than thirty muscles in my face and neck were working in concert as a dozen cranial nerves were busy zipping messages from those muscles to the pleasure centers of my brain—the right ventral tegmental and right caudate nucleus if you're keeping score—which woke up with a vengeance, probably for the first time since I'd been weaned off of methadone. I learned that Chey's kisses were causing the posterior lobe of my pituitary gland to release a hormone called oxytocin into my blood, filling me with feelings of generosity, social connectedness, and all over goodness. (Oxytocin is a drug that can turn any rational person into the village idiot, and is just crying out for someone to market it. Hey, FAP, maybe I should major in marketing!) And had I been paying attention, I would've noticed that my blood pressure and heart rate were spiking, my pupils were dilating, that I was getting seismic level cutis anserina (goose bumps), and that I was horripilating in the best possible way. (Some more SAT words for your reading pleasure.)

Interesting stuff, but pointless. The truth is, I was beyond reason, beyond thought. It was the closest thing to playing the guitar I'd ever experienced.

I can't find my own words to describe kissing Cheyenne, so I'll share a Chinese proverb we'd learned in tenth grade English:

Kissing is like drinking salted water
You drink, and your thirst increases

A total of five seconds later—though the concept of time had lost all meaning—something snapped Cheyenne back to the moment and she pulled away.

"Harry, I'm . . . I'm sorry."

Cheyenne got up and walked down the driveway.

She was gone.

I'M FREE

(written by Peter Townshend, and performed by The Who)

By the time we were supposed to go on, just after dark, it seemed like every kid in town was there. There were skate punks with shaved heads, alt rockers with untucked flannel shirts and ripped jeans, new wave kids with over-teased hair, even some thick-necked jocks from UGA. Every kid, except for Cheyenne.

"Dude," Richie asked me quietly, "do you think she followed Johnny home?"

I was just starting to wonder the same thing when Chey walked up with her bass slung across her back. She looked at both of us and said, "Let's play." She walked out onto the makeshift stage.

I was in my full Scar Boy getup—glasses, hat, denim jacket with the collar up (really uncomfortable in the Georgia heat)—ready to escape at the first sign of trouble, but there was no turning back.

Our opening song—"Girl in the Band"—began with the bass and drums pounding out an up-tempo four-four groove. As I waited for my cue, to thrash in the first chords from the guitar, I gave my body to the rhythm and started moving with the music. At first I tapped my foot, which is all I'd ever done onstage before that night, but within a few bars I was letting my whole body shake to the beat. And then the strangest thing happened. I heard a voice in my head.

Yeah, I know. Crazy. But it wasn't *that* kind of voice. The voice was mine; it was the voice I'd been hearing all my life, the voice that had recited list after boring list of presidents and baseball stats, the voice that had told me to keep quiet when other kids gave me a hard time, the voice that had always done what it was told. But that night I heard something in that voice I'd never heard before: The voice was smiling.

Pump your fist in the air, the voice suggested, so I did. It was a good idea. With each pump the crowd smacked their hands together, filling the night with thundering clap after thundering clap.

Introduce the band, the voice told me. I did that, too.

"On the drums, give it up for the skateboarding prince of the groove, Richie McGill!" The guys riding boards on the pipe behind Richie whooped and hollered. He took the cue and did an extended drum fill. The crowd went wild.

Throw your hat, the voice said. I took the hat off my head, leaving the wig intact, and threw it off the stage. It was snatched one-handed out of the air by a UGA co-ed. She managed to catch it without spilling a drop of her beer.

"On the bass, the princess of pounding rhythm, Cheyenne Belle." Some of the kids had flashlights and had been waving them in the air like light sabers. All at once they trained their light on Cheyenne. She was radiant. Again the audience screamed in delight.

I didn't need the voice to tell me what to do next. My jacket came off and I threw my sunglasses deep into the crowd. Then I threw my wig.

"And I'm Harbinger Robert Francis Jones, the king of darkness and despair, and . . ." Without prior arrangement, without even exchanging a glance, Richie and Chey came to a thundering halt in perfect unison. The echo of the last beat filled the yard and died. The flashlight-spotlight hit me, revealing every crevice of my scars in excruciating detail. There was an audible and collective gasp. In the nanosecond that I paused, I thought about running out of the yard and never looking back, about getting out of that god damn light.

I looked over at Richie and Chey and they were smiling at me. They were both sporting ear-to-ear grins, like that stupid cat in the comics. I knew I wasn't going anywhere.

"And we," I shouted, "are the Scar Boys!"

The beat started again, this time with my guitar, and the crowd went berserk. As I sang the first verse, the voice in my head gave a pat on the back. *Nice*, it said.

Thanks, I answered, and we were off and running.

I DON'T WANT TO KNOW

(written by Stevie Nicks, and performed by Fleetwood Mac)

Those few hours on the night of the Scar Boys fund-raiser were the best hours of my life. Nothing—and I mean nothing—will ever top them. Sure, adults blather on about their wedding days or holding their newborn children for the first time, or blah, blah, blah, blah. I don't care. That gig and that kiss were it. It was a climax, a zenith, the realization of a perfect crescendo. I was on the summit of Everest and I was walking on the moon. I wanted to live those moments over and over and over again. And now that we had money to finish the tour, and now that Cheyenne and I had connected, maybe, just maybe I could. My life finally felt like it was turning a corner, like all that awful shit I'd dealt with for all those years would just fade away like bad graffiti. The sunlight would finally win out.

Which is why it had to all come crashing down.

I don't remember what I did after the gig that night. I know that I drank, a lot, because I woke up the next morning with my head feeling like a pendulum's weight and throw-up stains on my shirt. I didn't even know if the stains were mine or someone else's. I didn't care.

I found Richie in our room, wearing a pair of socks and boxer shorts and smiling in his sleep. Penny Vick was lounging on the end of his bed smoking a cigarette.

"Great show, Harry," she said, offering me a smoke.

Penny was a pharmacology student at UGA who'd taken a shine to Richie. He was a little too dense to notice at first, but she'd been all over him like poison ivy the two days leading up to the fund-raiser, and from the looks of what I'd found in his bedroom, he'd finally caught on.

Everything about Penny was interesting and exciting. She had an eight-inch, spiked Mohawk that was blue the day we met her and flaming orange the night of the party. She read interesting books—John Fowles and Jim Carroll. She listened to cool music—R.E.M. and Hüsker Dü. She was the only girl I'd ever met who knew more world capitals, more geographical stats, and more useless trivia than me. (She told me she was an insomniac, and that the lists helped her sleep. Go figure.) Penny was also a constant fixture at the skate house. Her talent on the pipe was well established, and her ability to spar with the otherwise all-boys club— verbally, physically, and otherwise—was legendary.

We got to know Penny in those first few days nearly as well as we got to know Tony and Chuck. In some ways better, because Penny was smart. Really smart. She was in her second year at UGA and, according to Tony, was the "Queen of the Dean's List." She was fascinated with the Scar Boys and would pepper us with questions about our band and life in New York. Some of it, I figured, was just a way to get closer to Richie, but most of it was genuine.

"Thanks," I said, taking the cigarette and bending down for her light. "Is he going to wake up any time soon?" I asked.

"I doubt it." She smiled.

I shrugged my shoulders and went in search of Cheyenne. I couldn't find her anywhere, and none of the all-night party stragglers—about a dozen people had crashed at the skate house—had seen her. Chuck saw me milling about and handed me an envelope.

"Open it," he said, sounding serious. I peeked inside and saw a big, fat wad of cash. It smelled like beer, but it was legal tender. I looked up and Chuck was smiling. He watched me count out $1,627, mostly in tens, fives, and singles.

"Is this all for us?"

"Yeah, we took about a hundred out to cover our costs, but the rest is yours."

"Sixteen hundred dollars?"

"I know, right?" Chuck said.

We would be able to finish the tour. The Scar Boys were going out as a three-piece, and we were going to finish the tour. I didn't know what to say or do, so I just stood there for a long minute. And then, in the joy of the moment, I felt something I almost never felt: Spontaneous.

"Can you drive me out to where you think there are cars for sale?" I asked.

"Hell yeah," he answered.

An hour later I pulled into the driveway in a two-door, gray, 1976 Oldsmobile Omega. It had 100,000 miles on it and it seemed to run great. I probably should've waited for Richie and Cheyenne, but it was a steal, only three hundred dollars. That meant we'd have the rest of the money to stay in hotels and eat actual food.

When I returned to the skate house and stepped out of the car, I found that the Earth had moved.

Richie, Penny, and Chuck were sitting on the back stoop consoling Cheyenne, who was crying uncontrollably. Richie looked visibly shaken.

"What's wrong?" I asked.

"We had a call," Chuck began, and paused. An alarm bell went off in my head. It seemed like he didn't know how to continue. I waited. "It was from New York," he said. The alarm bell became an air-raid siren. "It's your friend, Johnny. There's been an accident."

DEAD MAN'S CURVE

(written by Jan Berry, Roger Christian, Arthur Kornfield, and Brian Wilson, and performed by Jan & Dean)

My first thought on hearing Johnny was in an accident was:
Serves him right.

I know, I know. I'm a complete and utter dick. But you have to look at it from my point of view. Everything about my life got better the moment Johnny McKenna exited stage left. And it wasn't just Cheyenne. Yes, connecting with her was awesome. But there was so much more. Without Johnny around to control my every move, without him to remind me, overtly or otherwise, that I needed to be cared for, that I could never be more than one of the sheep, I went through a kind of metamorphosis. It was finally my turn to become a butterfly. Strike that. Maybe it's better to say I became a moth. Either way, I was no longer the caterpillar, the sheep, the lackey, the number two. With Johnny gone, I was my own man.

It would be my wings flapping now and causing thunderstorms, or whatever else. It was freedom. Wonderful, wonderful freedom.

So yeah, there was a measure of satisfaction deep in my gut when I heard that Johnny'd been in an accident. I'm not saying I'm proud of it, but it's the truth.

Of course, if I probe deeper I can see that my years of kowtowing to Johnny weren't really his fault. They were my own fault. Every toady needs a boss and I was no different. We were symbionts. Fonzie and Richie. No wait. That's not right. Richie had too much moxie. Maybe Fonzie and Potsie. Huh, I guess I was the real Potsie all along. Anyway, after I thought about it for a minute, after I let my brain take over for my heart, I did feel bad. Just not as bad as I should have.

I listened as Richie told me the story:

Johnny had made it to New York by suppertime on that first day. He had taken a bus to Atlanta and used his cash to buy an airplane ticket. His parents met him at the airport and drove him home. It was later than usual for Johnny's evening run, but he told his mother that a lot had happened and he needed to clear his head.

The sky was already dark purple when Johnny walked out the door and quickened his step. With the moon in its new phase, it didn't take long for all the color to seep into the stars and for the night to turn black.

Johnny ran his usual route, up Colonial Parkway, up Underhill, across Grandview Boulevard, and down Alta Vista Drive. That's where the car hit him.

Alta Vista is a narrow road with lots of curves that ends in a steep hill. Even in the glow of a midday sun, it would be easy for a person on foot to get in the way of a car. On a moonless night, it's almost guaranteed.

Johnny ran that route often, and he knew how to listen for and look out for cars. I'm not sure how he found himself in a position where he couldn't get out of the way, but that's what happened.

The car slammed Johnny into a tree, pinning his right leg to the tree trunk. He managed to hold on to consciousness for the next twenty-five minutes, until an ambulance arrived. I have to believe that that was the worst part, the not passing out.

His leg from just below the right knee was hanging on by a stretch of skin and some ligaments. The bone had been completely fractured in two. I can't even begin to imagine what that pain was like.

Wait, strike that. Yes. Yes I can.

Johnny was rushed to the hospital where a team of doctors spent twelve excruciating hours trying to save the leg, only to amputate it in the end.

It was all too incredible to believe.

Chey stood, tears bubbling out of her eyes, but somehow

she kept her voice calm and steady. "I need to be alone," she said, and retreated to her bedroom.

Penny hugged Richie, and the two of them went inside. Chuck started to say something to me then thought better of it and stopped. He shrugged his shoulders and went inside, too, leaving me there alone. So I walked.

I don't really remember where I went or what I did. But I walked all day. By the time I got back to the house, the sun was going down and Chey was gone. She'd taken a third of the money we'd earned at the fund-raiser, taken her bass, and left us a note. It said, "Gone to see Johnny."

For the second time in my eighteen years, a random event was turning my life completely upside down. I had just begun to learn how to live with the first random event, the lightning strike, and now this. Now fucking this.

Yeah, this new thing hadn't happened to me, it had happened to Johnny. But that didn't seem to matter. Everything that was important to me was about to crumble away, again. If I ever felt cursed—and I'd spent a lot of my life feeling cursed—it was at that moment, standing in Athens, Georgia, holding Cheyenne's note.

GOING HOME

(written and performed by Mark Knopfler)

Johnny was hit by a twenty-one-year-old kid who had graduated our high school three years earlier. His name was Ronny Petrillo and he was so drunk that after he hit Johnny, he stumbled out of the car and passed out on the side of the road. It wasn't until someone else drove by and saw Johnny pinned between the car and the tree, and Ronny curled up on the asphalt like he was at home, snug in bed, that they called the police.

I remember Ronny. He was one of the cud-chewing cave trolls who attempted to rule the school with brute force. He and his gang wore leather jackets all day, every day, and kept unlit cigarettes behind their ears, like they'd watched *Welcome Back, Kotter* or *The Warriors* one too many times. There was an exchange student in their year, a quiet boy from Budapest, who they'd beat senseless just because he had a "funny" accent. Welcome to the USA, kid.

I'd had only one direct encounter with Ronny. In my freshman year I was standing outside the school, just sort of hanging out, like lots of kids do. I usually knew better. Guys like me have to keep moving. As soon as we stand still, we're easy targets. Kind of like gazelles on the Serengeti.

Anyway, I was standing in front of the school wearing a pair of sunglasses, when Ronny, then a senior, walked by. In one motion he took the sunglasses off my face, dropped them in his own path, crushed them with his next step, and kept walking. He wasn't with a group of friends, so there was no audience, and he never looked back at me. Of all the insult and injury I've suffered in my life, it is the clearest example of pure, undiluted malice I can recall. It was meanness without purpose.

When the police took Ronny away after he hit Johnny, he was so messed up that he stayed passed out on the car ride to the police station and all through the night. They couldn't read him his rights and book him until the next morning.

With Chey gone, there was nothing for Richie and me to do but go home. The sixteen-hour trip was the quietest car ride of my life. The only meaningful conversation we had lasted less than one minute and it took place just south of the Delaware Memorial Bridge.

"That really sucks about Johnny," Richie said.

"Yeah," I answered.

"Do you think he'll be okay?"

"I have no idea."

And that was it.

I could tell from the tone of Richie's voice that he was pretty freaked out. I would've tried to comfort him if I hadn't been so freaked out, too.

When we got back to Yonkers at one a.m., Richie dropped me at home and kept the car. We both figured that it made more sense for Richie and his dad to fix it up or sell it.

The moonless night had brewed a deep gloom in Colonial Heights, the neighborhood I called home. The shadows were so complete that while I could see the outline of my house when we pulled up, I couldn't see any detail. Not that there was much to see. I grew up in a nondescript split-level home; the outside a combination of white shingle and fake brick that must've been popular sometime in the 1950s or '60s because half the houses in the neighborhood looked pretty much the same.

The closest streetlamp, two houses down, cast just enough light for me to see the giant oak that rose from the edge of our driveway. The tree was old, probably older than the house itself, and its roots had been churning up the yard and front walk for as long as I could remember. I'd played with Matchbox cars and plastic army men in the nooks and crannies at the base of that tree when I was little, or so some old family photos have led me to believe.

That was before the lightning strike, before my memory circuits were fried.

I'd telephoned my parents when Richie and I left Athens to let them know I was coming home. It was the first time I'd called them since we left New York, and I could hear the relief in my mother's voice. It turns out they'd heard about Johnny and had been trying to reach me.

I crept into the house, figuring my folks would be asleep. They weren't. They were both on the landing just inside the front door. My mother had me in a bear hug before I could put my guitar down. It didn't take long until I was hugging her back and crying on her robe. I didn't know until that moment how much I'd missed my mom and how much everything hurt. When we finally let each other go, my dad wrapped his arms around me and held on tighter and longer than I thought he would or could.

It was good to be home.

I told my parents how tired I was and that I would catch them up on everything the next day. They said they understood and went back upstairs, and I went downstairs to my bedroom.

I don't know why I was surprised to see the room exactly as I'd left it. I'd been away less than a month, but it felt like I was walking into a museum exhibit. *Step right up and see the real live habitat of a late twentieth-century boy.* A Blondie poster, with Debbie Harry standing tall and lean in fishnet stockings stood watch over the twin bed, still made with New York Mets sheets. The shelves of the book-cases, loaded with comic books and science fiction novels, were sagging and looked ready to fall. And in one corner of the room, an old nylon-string acoustic guitar sat propped against the wall.

I flopped down on the creaking bed feeling like Gulliver. Everything in my life that had come before Athens seemed so small and distant. I fell into an uneasy sleep, tortured by a dream of having lost my guitar in the basement of the house in Georgia. Every time I thought I caught a glimpse of it, an army of jumping spiders blocked my way. When I woke late the next morning, I was disoriented. Part of me didn't know where I was, and part of me didn't know *when* I was.

My parents were camped out in the kitchen sharing the local newspaper when I entered. They both smiled at me and said hello. There was something wrong with their greeting. It was too nice, too forced. I stopped in my tracks.

"What's going on?"

"What?" my father asked. "Can't we just be happy to see you?"

I looked at them both for a long moment. "No," I said.

"Harry," my mother began, "Dr. Hirschorn called us."

Of course. Dr. Kenny. After my late-night, deranged call from the phone booth in Athens, Dr. Kenny had called my parents. Ugh.

"We'd like you to start seeing him again," my father added. "We'll pay for it, of course." I thought maybe there was a tinge of resentment in his offer to pay. But maybe I imagined it, too. Something about my dad looked broken, defeated. The lines on his face seemed deeper, his hairline looked higher on his forehead.

A lot flashed through my mind. I thought about the sessions with Dr. Kenny from when I was younger and how much they helped me. I wondered if his office was still the same. I wondered if eighteen-year-olds were even allowed to see pediatric psychiatrists, I wondered if he would put me on meds. But with all those thoughts crashing through my brain, I couldn't think of a good reason to say no. So I said nothing.

"We've made an appointment for you for next Wednesday," my father added. He looked like he didn't have any fight left in him. I probably could've refused the appointment with Dr. Kenny, but the truth is, I didn't have any fight left in me either.

I shrugged my shoulders and nodded agreement.

I had that conversation with my parents on a Friday. I spent the next few days lounging around the house, eating sugar-coated cereal, watching sitcom reruns on television, and trying not to think about anything. Other than my mom and dad, I talked to no one. Not even Richie, who'd called a couple of times. I think I needed to detox.

I didn't even play the guitar. Every time I had the urge, I'd look at the guitar case and be reminded of too much bad crap. I didn't know if I'd ever play again.

TIME'S UP

(written by Howard Devoto and Pete Shelley, and performed by the Buzzcocks)

4

Dr. Kenny and I picked up right where we'd left off five years earlier—me on the couch staring up at the Sharpie drawings of rock stars that lined his office walls, and Kenny in the big comfy chair at my side, leaning forward with his elbows on his knees.

The couch felt like a bit of a cliché. You see it in every hackneyed movie or television show about psychiatry. But when I first began my appointments as an eight-year-old, I was so physically weak from the trauma of my ordeal that lying down was easier than sitting up, and the couch became my spot. Old habits die hard, I guess.

While the whole experience felt very familiar to me, some things had changed, too. Most notably, Dr. Kenny.

The streaks of gray that had flecked the black hair at Dr. Kenny's temples when I was younger were now peppered across his entire head. But it wasn't just the hair that made him seem older. There was a sadness about Dr. Kenny that hadn't been there before. Like the world had beaten him down. His insides had gone from the warm glow of halogen light to the cold glare of fluorescence. The best way to describe the Dr. Kenny from my youth was the Iggy Pop song "Lust for Life"; now he seemed to fit better with Frank Sinatra's "That's Life" instead.

I'd noticed a similar thing with my dad, and it made me wonder if people, when they reach a certain age, forget how to be happy. Like maybe they grow up to become what they were once rebelling against, and it makes them sad without even knowing it.

I asked Dr. Kenny about the sadness at our second session. I was still getting him caught up on everything that'd happened to me since I'd "abandoned him"—his words, not mine—but his attention seemed to wander. I asked if he was okay.

"You really want to know?" he asked.

I nodded.

"I lost a patient two years ago," he said. He must've seen me look perplexed, because he added, "Suicide."

Dr. Kenny is a gentle and sensitive soul. I can't begin to imagine how that would've made him feel. No wonder he was so freaked out by my phone call from Athens.

"Do you want to talk about it?" I asked. Dr. Kenny

looked at me like he'd never seen me before. And that's the other thing that had changed about our relationship: Me.

I was broken almost beyond repair when Dr. Kenny and I found one another in 1976, and our bond developed as one of teacher and student. Much like my relationship with Johnny or my father, I was beta to Dr. Kenny's alpha, though in a far more loving and constructive way. He asked the questions, I evaded the answers.

But that kid was gone, replaced by an older, more complicated Harbinger Jones. That this new model had the wherewithal, the balls, to ask a direct and caring question like, "Do you want to talk about it?" must've thrown Dr. Kenny for a loop.

"Thanks, Harry," he finally said. "I really appreciate that, but I can't violate doctor-patient confidentiality."

"Even if the patient is . . . gone?"

"Even if the patient is gone," he answered, choking on the word.

"Huh," I grunted in response. He grunted, too.

I told Dr. Kenny everything. From Dave's odd disappearance from the band, to meeting Cheyenne, to cutting a record, to buying a van, to seeing Johnny and Cheyenne do it, to everything that happened in Georgia. I omitted nothing. It took me nearly three sessions to get it all out.

"And that brings us to the here and now, Dr. K," I said near the end of my third visit.

Dr. Kenny had stayed on the edge of his chair through my whole narrative, only interrupting when he needed to ask a question or clarify a point. He looked at me for a long moment when I finished, then sat back, took off his glasses, cleaned them, put them back on, and then looked at me some more. I knew this trick. He was trying to get me to say the one thing I wasn't saying. It almost always worked. But not this time. I really didn't know what the one thing was.

Then Dr. Kenny surprised me. Strike that. He blew me right out of the god damn water.

"You know, Harry," he said, "sometimes you can be such a schmuck."

The only time Dr. Kenny had ever said anything remotely like this to me was when I was twelve years old. For something like our fifth straight session I was coming in with schoolyard bruises to show him, visible reminders that socially I was lower than a pariah and only barely higher than a corpse. In fact, that's exactly what I told Dr. Kenny.

"Socially I'm lower than a pariah and only barely higher than a corpse."

I was kind of pleased with that line. I'd thought of it earlier in the week and had been waiting for my session with Dr. Kenny to use it. Apparently, it didn't play very well.

"Dammit, Harry," he'd said. Dr. Kenny never swore with me. "Don't you ever stand up for yourself?"

I was stunned into complete silence. Dr. Kenny ran his hands through the shaggy mop on his head and immediately apologized. I'm not sure what prompted him to go so far off his script. Was he stressed over stuff in his personal life? Problems with another patient? Had he just had enough of me? Whatever it was, it hurt. It took another two sessions to coax me back out of my shell.

But calling me a "schmuck" was different. I could tell Dr. Kenny was using the expression the same way he might use it with his own friends. I could also tell there would be no apology.

"Seriously," he continued, "just listen to yourself."

"What?" I wanted to sound indignant, but I don't think I pulled it off.

"You've been playing guitar in a rock band, you have friends, you kissed a girl, you've been traveling, you put out your own record. Most kids would give their big toe to live the life you're living."

"They can have it," I said almost reflexively.

Dr. Kenny rolled his eyes in exasperation. I'm not sure why I wasn't hearing Dr. Kenny. Whether it was a choice or not, I really couldn't say. He shook his head and decided to change tactics.

"How long have you been home now?" he asked.

"I dunno, about a month, I guess."

"And you haven't tried to talk to Johnny or Cheyenne?"

"No," I said to my shoes. "They hate me."

"How do you know that?"

"Haven't you been listening? Because the last time I saw Johnny we got in a fight and I hit him in the face." I'd told Kenny about my last encounter with Johnny, but hadn't used the word "slapped." I was still too embarrassed. "And now he only has one leg. And because I'm sure Cheyenne knows all about it, too. And because they both think it's my fault."

"How can you possibly know that?" I shrugged my shoulders. "Have you even talked to Richie?"

"No."

"Why?"

I shrugged again.

"And you're not playing your guitar?"

I shook my head.

"Don't you see?" There was such anguish in his voice that I looked up. "You're shutting yourself off from all the things—maybe the only things—that can help you move past this. You need to talk to Johnny and Cheyenne, Harry. And for fuck's sake, pick up your god damn guitar."

I started to protest, but Dr. Kenny waved me away in disgust. "Time's up."

Stunned into disbelief, I shuffled out of his office.

WE CAN WORK IT OUT

(written by John Lennon and Paul McCartney, and performed by the Beatles)

When I got home that afternoon, I opened my guitar case and stared at my Strat. It was a sleek guitar with an all-black body, a black pick guard, and a maple neck and fret board. I'd covered the beast with stickers acquired at various gigs—a skull and crossbones, Scooby-Doo, The Clash—which were already starting to peel and flake. There was a deep gouge next to the volume pot, the injury a reminder of smashing the guitar into Richie's ride cymbal on stage at the Bitter End. The mark was a badge of honor.

I wanted to pick the guitar up, but something was stopping me. It was like touching it would rip a hole in the fabric of space and time and catapult me backward to a place I didn't want to be. I closed the case and used my foot to nudge the whole thing under my bed. Like it was diseased.

Even though I couldn't bring myself to play the guitar,

I knew Dr. Kenny was right. I was being a real dick. Everything I'd wanted had been laid at my feet, and all I'd ever done was complain and feel sorry for myself. Maybe that's the way I was wired and I couldn't do anything else. But maybe I could.

I decided to call Richie.

"Dude!" he answered when he heard my voice. "Where the fuck you been?"

"Just kind of hanging around," I said. "How're you doing?"

Richie spent the next ten minutes describing every last detail of his new skateboard—its length, the kind of wheels it had, the paisley pattern on its underside—as well as the time he'd spent hanging out with the local skate punks and riding an improvised pipe in Valhalla. Turns out he'd been bit by the skateboarding bug when we were in Athens and couldn't shake it.

"You playing drums?" I asked, when he finished.

'Yeah, of course. That and killing time until school starts."

"I'm kind of jealous you get to go back to high school."

Richie laughed. "You hated that place."

"Yeah, well, the devil you know."

We made a plan to get together that coming weekend and were about to hang up when Richie asked, "So have you been to see Johnny yet?"

"No," I said, "I'm pretty sure he won't want to see me."

"I don't know, Harry," he answered. "The dude's in pretty bad shape. He wound up not going up to Syracuse. He's talking like he's never gonna go."

I wasn't surprised to hear that. Trauma is great at changing plans.

"A visit might do him good," Richie added.

Not knowing what else to say, I muttered, "Okay," and we said good-bye.

I knew that the growing chorus—Richie's voice now added to Dr. Kenny's and to my parents'—was right, that I really did need to go see Johnny. Problem is, I didn't want to. It didn't take a genius to figure out that I was scared, that I felt responsible for everything that'd happened. But I wasn't a genius (and even though I know admitting this won't help me get into your college, I can tell you that I'm still not a genius), and I can be thick as molasses when I want to. So if you had asked me back then, I would've told you that I didn't want to see Johnny because I didn't care about him. *Not* because I was afraid.

Cheyenne was a different story. I was definitely afraid of seeing her. I didn't want to let the universe taint the memory of our kiss or of the gig at the fund-raiser. They were the only things holding me together since we'd left Athens, and I was wrapping them in a protective cocoon. But the universe, as I seem destined to learn again and again, has a funny way of changing the story.

The day after talking to Richie I decided to go for a walk. A long walk. A walk like the one I took that night in Athens.

I moved with the energy of an over-wound toy and did everything I could to think about nothing. I tried counting states and listing presidents. I went through the periodic table and Triple Crown winners (baseball *and* horse racing). I calculated that with sixty-two years left (if I made my life expectancy), I had a mere fifteen presidential elections, Olympics, or World Cups left to enjoy; only seven hundred and fifty full moons to admire; just over three thousand two hundred *New York Times* Sunday crossword puzzles to attempt; less than twenty-three thousand mornings to open my eyes; and fewer than two billion beats left in my heart, a large but horrifyingly finite number. I was starting to freak myself out, so I shifted gears and listed every Academy Award Best Picture nominee in reverse chronological order. (The fact that *Chariots of Fire* beat out *Raiders of the Lost Ark* is still one of the great crimes of the twentieth century.) By the time I got to *Mutiny on the Bounty* (1935) I'd reached a small lake on the Yonkers-Bronxville border and I had started to calm down.

The lake was a three-quarter-mile long oval ringed by a dirt path, and it was one of my favorite places to go and think. The north end was marked by a grass field that butted up against a residential street, the south end by a footbridge that crossed from one side to the other at the narrowest point. That's where I stumbled on Cheyenne.

She was standing on the footbridge, staring into the small waterfall that tumbled out of the lake and into a narrow stream. The white foam of water was quickly calming itself for the journey into the heart of Bronxville.

I had my head down, mumbling the names of long-forgotten movies, when I rounded a corner and stepped onto the bridge. I looked up and saw Cheyenne, but she didn't see me.

Something about her had changed. It was like all the muscles in her face had lost their tension, giving her a pronounced droop.

I froze. My first instinct was to turn and run, and I almost did. But something made me stay. I watched her for a minute and then cleared my throat.

Chey didn't turn her head, but her face got that look people's faces get when they're really annoyed. Like when you're in a bad mood because you just know that your English teacher is going to give you a surprise quiz on the book you didn't read, and then he walks into the room and announces that there will indeed be a test. That's the look Cheyenne had, that "god damn it, I knew it," look.

"Hi Chey." I took a tentative stop forward.

"Not now, Harry. Just leave me alone."

"I just—"

Cheyenne turned and walked off the other side of the footbridge and onto the dirt path. I was stymied. I'd been pretty sure she was mad at me, but this was more than I'd expected. I was going to turn and leave the way I came, but I kept hearing Dr. Kenny's voice in my head saying, "You are such a schmuck, Harry," and Johnny's voice saying, "You are such a pussy." I had no choice but to press on.

I followed a few paces behind until Chey sat down on a park bench. I sat, too. I expected her to get up, but she didn't. She tucked her knees up to her chest and made herself as small as she possibly could. I didn't know if she was trying to hide from me or from the whole world.

I slid down the bench a bit and put my hand on her shoulder, like I had done on the stoop in Athens. I didn't think she could tense up anymore, but she did. At least she didn't flinch.

I didn't know what to say, but I was feeling an indescribable pressure to say something, so I started in the obvious place.

"Chey, I love you."

Yeah, I know, what the hell was I thinking? Somehow I thought saying it would make everything okay.

It didn't.

She threw up on my shoes.

When she was done retching, Cheyenne wiped her arm on her sleeve and started to get up. I pulled her gently back down.

"Wait," I said, "please, I'm sorry. I'm really sorry."

"No, Harry, I'm sorry."

"You're sorry? For what?"

"For kissing you." She started to cry, and this time she didn't tense up or pull away. She buried her head in my shoulder.

Cheyenne cried hard, covering my shirt with snot and tears. In between sobs and gasps she told me how dumb she was, how she should have listened to Johnny, how she should have left with him, how she could have stopped the whole thing, how he lost his leg and it was all her fault.

"He won't even see me, Harry," she said, starting to calm down.

"What?" I was not expecting *that*.

"He won't talk to me on the phone, either. And you know his parents. They never liked me or you or the band, so they're not telling me anything. Has he said anything to you?"

"I haven't been to see him yet."

She looked at me with a blank expression and then nodded. I had no idea what she was thinking. We were both quiet for a few minutes.

"What should I do?" Her question was so tortured that it made my heart hurt. It felt terrible and I blurted out something I probably shouldn't have. "I'll talk to him," I promised.

Chey smiled. It wasn't a broad smile, or a smile filled

with light and joy. It wasn't even really a happy smile. But it was a smile.

And written in that smile was the knowledge that she and I could never be more than friends. Cheyenne and Johnny were bound to each other, and even if the bond between them was to break, it was a fixed barrier between us, for then and for all time. I'm not going to lie and tell you that knowing this made everything feel any better. It didn't. But one thing I've learned, you can't hide from the truth, and there's no point in trying. I didn't say anything then, but I think I probably let out a whopping big sigh.

"Walk me home?" she said.

I nodded.

We didn't talk much on the way back, but the silence didn't bother me. Right then, all I wanted in the world was company.

When we got to Chey's door I mumbled good-bye and started to walk away. She grabbed my arm and hugged me. "I'm sorry, Harry. About everything. Let's try to start over, okay?"

And you know what? It *was* okay. I hugged her back and headed home.

NO SURRENDER

(written by Bruce Springsteen, and performed by Bruce Springsteen and the E Street Band)

It was late the following afternoon when I mustered the courage to visit Johnny. The promise I'd made to Chey was the final push I needed.

I wasn't scared about seeing Johnny's amputated leg. When I was younger and going through all kinds of rehabilitation, I spent lots of time in waiting rooms with amputees.

There was this one kid, about my age, who decided to introduce himself to me.

"Hi, I'm Stumpy Joe." I must've looked at him cross-eyed, because he laughed and said, "Nah, that's not really my name, but it breaks the ice. My real name is George. What's your name?"

As usual, I was frozen and couldn't think of a response. Not even my name. I guess he figured that I was both deformed and a bit challenged, because he turned to the kid sitting on the other side of him and said, "Hi, I'm Stumpy Joe."

So missing arms, missing hands, missing legs weren't anything new to me. Seeing Johnny's stump wasn't going to be a problem.

It was the rest of him that was making me nervous. The part of him that would remember that I was the guy who'd hit (slapped) him, and that I was the guy who'd started the chain of events that ended with his leg on an operating room floor.

When I rang the doorbell, Mrs. McKenna—a tumbler of brown, translucent, and potent-smelling liquid in her hand—greeted me cordially, which was all she'd ever done. Johnny's parents wished he'd hung out with a better class of friends, and given how things turned out, you can't really blame them.

The cubes of ice were clinking against the sides of her glass and echoing through the hall as she escorted me to Johnny's bedroom door. She put a hand on my shoulder and said, "See if you can help him, Harry." The tone in her voice suggested no else had been able to. She walked away down the hall and I went in.

I found Johnny sitting up in bed, the covers pulled to his waist, his missing leg hidden from view. He was reading a weathered, library copy of *The Catcher in the Rye* and looked up when I entered. He didn't smile.

"Hey," I said. Johnny nodded in response. "How're you doing?" He shrugged his shoulders. I sat down on the edge of his bed.

I saw something in Johnny that I hadn't seen in a long time. A decade, to be exact. Written in the creases of Johnny's brow, in the glass sheen of his eyes, in the tension in his neck and back, on his foul breath, in the dirty pajamas he wore, in his unkempt and uncut hair, and across the expanse of clutter in his room—written in every fiber of Johnny's being was the same agony I'd felt after the thunderstorm. He was trapped in the disaster of himself and couldn't find a way out.

Seeing him sitting there, seeing *myself* sitting there, I realized that I'd never left that place. And suddenly, I felt like a fool. Like the biggest god damn fool on the god damn face of the god damn Earth. This is what Dr. Kenny had been trying to tell me. That I was a fool. I was such a fool that I had to laugh out loud.

"Jesus, Harry, did you come here to laugh at me?" Johnny's face was turning red.

"What? Oh, no, no. I was thinking of something someone said to me a long time ago, after the lightning strike." His posture relaxed. He waited for me to continue.

"Do you know anything about Chinese butterflies?"

I don't know if I did Lucky's story justice, or if it helped, but it was enough of a distraction to allow Johnny to loosen up. He asked me questions about the day Lucky came to see me, and for the first time in a long time, we just talked, like we used to, before, well, before everything.

After a while there was a break in the conversation, so I steeled my nerve and said, "Johnny, I saw Cheyenne."

At the mention of Chey's name the temperature in the room dropped fifteen degrees.

Johnny looked darts at me. "What about Chey," he said. My first thought was that he somehow knew that she and I had kissed, but I couldn't imagine how so I pressed on.

"She thinks you hate her."

"Good."

"What?"

He nodded to the blanket, his hidden wound meant to serve as an exclamation point.

"I don't understand," I said.

"I'm letting her off the hook. I don't want her pity, and I don't want her to have to settle for someone who isn't all here." He threw his book onto the blanket, landing it in the spot where his leg should have been. He did it to make me uncomfortable, but it didn't work. Johnny had lots of weapons against me; disfigurement wasn't one of them.

"I don't understand."

"You said that already."

"If you didn't want to see any of us, why did your mom call Athens to tell us you were in the accident in the first place?"

"Who said I didn't want to see any of you?"

"I don't under—"

"You don't understand. Yeah, so I've gathered. Look, Harry, I'm not sure if I told my mom to call the skate house, or if it was her idea. That was like less than two days after my surgery"—he nearly gagged on the word—"and I was so full of morphine you could've, oh, I don't know, *slapped me in the face* and I wouldn't have felt it."

Ouch, I thought.

"And it wasn't the band I wanted to get in touch with, it was you, Harry. You!" His cheeks were the color of an apple and he was short of breath. "Where the fuck have you been?" he shouted at me.

I didn't know what to say. I didn't know what to think. "I'm sorry," I muttered. "I thought you were mad at me, because I hit you."

"Slapped me," he corrected.

"Slapped you," I admitted.

"I *was* mad at you, Harry. But then this happened," he said, pointing to his leg, "and somehow the slap in the face didn't seem so bad."

"But I still don't understand," I said. "Then why didn't you call me?"

"You were supposed to call me!" he said, his voice rising again.

"You're right, you're right," I said, hands up and out in

a sign of surrender, hoping to calm him down. "I'm really sorry, John. I really am. But I'm here now."

No response. I let a long moment pass. Maybe I'd been wrong. Maybe I'd been judging Johnny through a lens of jealousy. And not just jealousy about Cheyenne, jealousy about everything he was and I was not. Maybe it was me who'd been the crappy friend.

But something was still bothering me. "I still don't understand," I said quietly.

He rolled his eyes. "What?"

"Why you don't want to see Cheyenne."

"I told you. I'm doing her a favor."

"But she loves you."

"Which is why I need to push her away. Do you think I like doing this?"

"Then don't."

No response.

"You know, John, sometimes you can be one stubborn, arrogant prick." As I think I've established, this isn't the kind of thing I was used to saying to Johnny, and it wasn't the kind of thing he was used to hearing from me. But seeing him there helped me understand how the world saw me and that was like a tonic. For once, I could be the other guy. I could be Kung Fu.

"Be careful, Harry." He didn't even try to hide the anger in his voice. I ignored it.

"Dude, you're my best friend." This hung in the air for a second. I think it surprised us both. "And you're the luckiest guy in the world to have a girl like Cheyenne. I'd give anything for that. I almost did. Don't blow it."

"Luckiest guy in the world? Are you out of your mind? Look at me!"

"I am looking, John."

"You're looking but you're not seeing! This is not lucky!" He pulled the blanket back, exposing his stump. His pajama bottoms were tied up in a knot, hiding the wound, but that didn't lessen the impact of the visual. "I'm a cripple, a gimp, a freak! How the fuck would you know anything about what I feel!" He screamed so loud I thought a window might shatter. I let his words ricochet around the room, bounce off his stereo, zigzag through his books, rattle the lightbulbs in the matching bedside lamps, careen off the poster of 1972 Olympics marathoner Frank Shorter, bounce off the worn carpet, shoot back up, and explode off the ceiling, until they were falling down on his head like soft rain.

He looked up at me, and he saw me. He really saw me. His shoulders sagged, and he nodded, realizing that I was the only person in his entire world who knew exactly how he felt.

"Just talk to her, okay?" I said quietly.

Johnny nodded again.

The shoe of our conversations had been so long on the other foot—with Johnny schooling me, and me setting my jaw and taking it—that neither one of us knew what to say next. Or maybe we'd both said what we'd needed to say, and we were worn out.

Either way, I couldn't really look at Johnny so I let my eye wander the room.

There was a new acoustic guitar—a sunburst Takamine with a built-in pickup—propped against the wall opposite the bed. Johnny saw me eyeing it.

"Go ahead," he said, I think relieved as much as I was, to change the subject. "My parents bought it to cheer me up. I haven't touched it."

I took the guitar, more as a defense against further angst than anything else, sat down cross-legged on the floor, and started strumming and picking random notes. The guitar felt heavy in my hands, but not like a weight. It was like an anchor, rooting me safely to the spot. It was like morphine, replacing so much pain with so much euphoria. People would come and people would go, I realized then, but music would be there until the end of time. (Note to self: Never question Dr. Kenny again. The guy is almost always right.)

I let that thought, about music, wash over me as I started to absentmindedly strum the chords of a song Johnny and I had been working on before we left to go on tour.

A to A7, A to A7.

I was playing soft but with a quick tempo. I let the simple chord progression drone on, the sound of it filling Johnny's room with the joy that only an acoustic guitar can bring. Just before I was about to shift to the chords in the bridge, Johnny surprised me and started to sing along.

You give a little and take a lot
As distant guns are echoing shots
You never find the time to stop
You just keep reaching for the top
And you think you're walking a thin line but you're not
Able to see what's at stake

You had your chance
To do your time
To rectify
Your useless crimes
But don't worry
No one noticed

Your eyes are flooded with gin
Your head is needles and pins
Knee deep in original sin
Everything just started to spin
Someone had better notify your next of kin that you might not
make it

You had your chance
To do your time
To rectify
Your useless crimes
But don't worry
No one noticed.

We looked at each other as the last chord faded out, both cautious. It was Johnny who let his guard down first.

"You know," he said, "the name of this band will make a lot more sense now that there are two of us." He paused a beat, and we both burst out laughing. We laughed like that until we both cried.

When we were both tired and dried out, I started to strum chords to another Scar Boys song. Johnny pitched forward, ready to sing the first verse.

Music to the rescue again.

THE SONG IS OVER

(written by Peter Townshend, and performed by The Who)

I wasn't sure what I wanted to accomplish when I sat down to write this essay. Strike that. I know exactly what I wanted to accomplish. I wanted you, Faceless Admissions Professional, to know who I was. You were never going to get that from SAT scores, my GPA, and a two-hundred-and fifty-word essay.

That day in Johnny's room was nearly six months ago. He never went off to Syracuse and I don't think he ever will. The four of us have been jamming again, and it's been great. I'm not sure where it will lead, but this time I understand that it's not where I end up that matters, but how I get there.

The truth is, while I know I'm supposed to want to go to college, that everyone is supposed to want to go to college, following the pack has never worked out all that well for me. I only filled out your application to please my parents. After everything that happened, it seemed like the right thing to do. What I want is to play music. If you've read this far, you've probably figured that out. But, did you read this far? I doubt it. And that's okay. The exercise has been its own reward.

I started out telling you I was a coward, and I probably still am. But maybe I've learned something else here, too. I finally know who I am. I'm no longer the shy ugly kid with the scars. I'm the shy ugly kid with the scars who plays guitar, who loves music, and who has friends. And you know what? That's good enough for me.

ACKNOWLEDGMENTS

This book would simply not exist with the love, support, input, feedback, advice, pushing, prodding, cheering—and did I mention love?—of my best friend, live-in editor, and oh yeah, my wife, Kristen Gilligan Vlahos. Without Krissy, I'd still be writing really bad screenplays in the basement.

Carl Lennertz, Allison Hill, and Sarah Darer Littman were all early champions of *The Scar Boys*; without their editorial input and encouragement, I'd still be writing really bad poetry in the attic.

There were far too many readers of various drafts of *The Scar Boys*, all of whom provided valuable feedback, for me to remember and name, but I'll give it a shot. Thank you to Stephanie Anderson, John Bohman, Tom Gilligan, Bobbi Gilligan, Tommy Gilligan, Richard Hunt, Grandwinnie Kalassay, Kathy Leydon, Lauren McCartney, Karen Schechner, Nadine Vassallo and, and . . . damn, I'm very sorry if I forgot to include you here. Without your collective help, I'd still be writing really bad polemics on the patio. (Yeah, okay, this joke is already stale.)

My outstanding agent, Sandra Bond, never wavered in her faith in this project; and Greg Ferguson, my brilliant editor at Egmont, understood this story from the beginning. His keen insight made *The Scar Boys* a better book at every turn. I am indebted to both. And thank you to Andrea Cascardi, Margaret Coffee, and the entire team at Egmont for their incredible, and incredibly smart, support.

Thank you to my parents for instilling in me a love of the written word. Thank you, Oren Teicher and everyone at ABA, for the ceaseless encouragement and support, especially Mark Nichols. Thank you, Chris Finan, for all the good writing advice.

I've had the pleasure to know many wonderful booksellers throughout the course of my life. Six of the most extraordinary—Becky Anderson, Cathy Berner, Valerie Koehler, Collette Morgan, Matt Norcross, and Andrea Vuleta—were instrumental in helping this book find a home.

And last, but not least, thanks to the real Woofing Cookies: Joe Loskywitz, Scott Nafz, and Chad Strohmayer. The adventures we had together as kids formed the backdrop of Harry's tale. This story is their story as much as it is my own. Their friendship has and will always mean the world to me.

LEN VLAHOS

dropped out of NYU film school at age 19 to go on the road with a touring punk/pop band called the Woofing Cookies, which eventually became the backdrop for *The Scar Boys*. He now works in the book industry and lives with his wife and two children in Connecticut. You can visit him online at www.lenvlahos.com and follow him on Facebook and Twitter @LenVlahos.